A Book of Burlesques

H. L. Mencken

A Book of Burlesques

The present edition is a reproduction of previous publication of this classic work. Minor typographical errors may have been corrected without note; however, for an authentic reading experience the spelling, punctuation, and capitalization have been retained from the original text.

ISBN: 978-1-64799-983-4

CONTENTS

Chapters

The present edition includes some epigrams from "A Little Book in C Major," now out of print. To make room for them several of the smaller sketches in the first edition have been omitted. Nearly the whole contents of the book appeared originally in The Smart Set. The references to a Europe not yet devastated by war and an America not yet polluted by Prohibition show that some of the pieces first saw print in far better days than these.

H. L. M.
February 1, 1920

I

Death

A Philosophical Discussion

The back parlor of any average American home. The blinds are drawn and a single gas-jet burns feebly. A dim suggestion of festivity: strange chairs, the table pushed back, a decanter and glasses. A heavy, suffocating, discordant scent of flowers—roses, carnations, lilies, gardenias. A general stuffiness and mugginess, as if it were raining outside, which it isn't.

A door leads into the front parlor. It is open, and through it the flowers may be seen. They are banked about a long black box with huge nickel handles, resting upon two folding horses. Now and then a man comes into the front room from the street door, his shoes squeaking hideously. Sometimes there is a woman, usually in deep mourning. Each visitor approaches the long black box, looks into it with ill-concealed repugnance, snuffles softly, and then backs of toward the door. A clock on the mantelpiece ticks loudly. From the street come the usual noises—a wagon rattling, the clang of a trolley car's gong, the shrill cry of a child.

In the back parlor six pallbearers sit upon chairs, all of them bolt upright, with their hands on their knees. They are in their Sunday clothes, with stiff white shirts. Their hats are on the floor beside their chairs. Each wears upon his lapel the gilt badge of a fraternal order, with a crêpe rosette. In the gloom they are indistinguishable; all of them talk in the same strained, throaty whisper. Between their remarks they pause, clear their throats, blow their noses, and shuffle in their chairs. They are intensely

1

uncomfortable. Tempo: Adagio lamentoso, with occasionally a rise to andante maesto. So:

FIRST PALLBEARER

Who woulda thought that *he* woulda been the next?

SECOND PALLBEARER

Yes; you never can tell.

THIRD PALLBEARER

(*An oldish voice, oracularly.*) We're here to-day and gone to-morrow.

FOURTH PALLBEARER

I seen him no longer ago than Chewsday. He never looked no better. Nobody would have— —

FIFTH PALLBEARER

I seen him Wednesday. We had a glass of beer together in the Huffbrow Kaif. He was laughing and cutting up like he always done.

FIRST PALLBEARER

You never know who it's gonna hit next. Him and me was pallbearers together for Hen Jackson no more than a month ago, or say five weeks.

FIRST PALLBEARER

Well, a man is lucky if he goes off quick. If I had *my* way I wouldn't want no better way.

2

SECOND PALLBEARER

My brother John went thataway. He dropped like a stone, settin' there at the supper table. They had to take his knife out of his hand.

THIRD PALLBEARER

I had an uncle to do the same thing, but without the knife. He had what they call appleplexy. It runs in my family.

FOURTH PALLBEARER

They say it's in *his'n*, too.

FIFTH PALLBEARER

But he never looked it.

FIRST PALLBEARER

No. Nobody woulda thought *he* woulda been the next.

FIRST PALLBEARER

Them are the things you never can tell anything about.

SECOND PALLBEARER

Ain't it true!

THIRD PALLBEARER

We're here to-day and gone to-morrow.

(*A pause. Feet are shuffled. Somewhere a door bangs.*)

FOURTH PALLBEARER

(*Brightly.*) He looks elegant. I hear he never suffered none.

FIFTH PALLBEARER

No; he went too quick. One minute he was alive and the next minute he was dead.

FIRST PALLBEARER

Think of it: dead so quick!

FIRST PALLBEARER

Gone!

SECOND PALLBEARER

Passed away!

THIRD PALLBEARER

Well, we all have to go *some* time.

FOURTH PALLBEARER

Yes; a man never knows but what his turn'll come next.

FIFTH PALLBEARER

You can't tell nothing by looks. Them sickly fellows generally lives to be old.

FIRST PALLBEARER

Yes; the doctors say it's the big stout person that goes off the soonest. They say typhord never kills none but the healthy.

FIRST PALLBEARER

So I have heered it said. My wife's youngest brother weighed 240 pounds. He was as strong as a mule. He could lift a sugar-barrel, and then some. Once I seen him drink damn near a whole keg of beer. Yet it finished him in less'n three weeks—and *he* had it mild.

SECOND PALLBEARER

It seems that there's a lot of it this fall.

THIRD PALLBEARER

Yes; I hear of people taken with it every day. Some say it's the water. My brother Sam's oldest is down with it.

FOURTH PALLBEARER

I had it myself once. I was out of my head for four weeks.

FIFTH PALLBEARER

That's a good sign.

FIRST PALLBEARER

Yes; you don't die as long as you're out of your head.

FIRST PALLBEARER

It seems to me that there is a lot of sickness around this year.

SECOND PALLBEARER

I been to five funerals in six weeks.

THIRD PALLBEARER

I beat you. I been to six in five weeks, not counting this one.

FOURTH PALLBEARER

A body don't hardly know what to think of it scarcely.

5

FIFTH PALLBEARER

That.rss what *I* always say: you can't tell who'll be next.

FIRST PALLBEARER

Ain't it true! Just think of *him*.

FIRST PALLBEARER

Yes; nobody woulda picked *him* out.

SECOND PALLBEARER

Nor my brother John, neither.

THIRD PALLBEARER

Well, what *must* be *must* be.

FOURTH PALLBEARER

Yes; it don't do no good to kick. When a man's time comes he's got to go.

FIFTH PALLBEARER

We're lucky if it ain't us.

FIRST PALLBEARER

So I always say. We ought to be thankful.

FIRST PALLBEARER

That's the way *I* always feel about it.

SECOND PALLBEARER

It wouldn't do *him* no good, no matter *what* we done.

THIRD PALLBEARER

We're here to-day and gone to-morrow.

FOURTH PALLBEARER

But it's hard all the same.

FIFTH PALLBEARER

It's hard on *her*.

FIRST PALLBEARER

Yes, it is. Why should *he* go?

FIRST PALLBEARER

It's a question nobody ain't ever answered.

SECOND PALLBEARER

Nor never won't.

THIRD PALLBEARER

You're right there. I talked to a preacher about it once, and even *he* couldn't give no answer to it.

FOURTH PALLBEARER

The more you think about it the less you can make it out.

FIFTH PALLBEARER

When I seen him last Wednesday he had no more ideer of it than what you had.

7

FIRST PALLBEARER

Well, if I had *my* choice, that's the way I would always want to die.

FIRST PALLBEARER

Yes; that's what *I* say. I am with you there.

SECOND PALLBEARER

Yes; you're right, both of you. It don't do no good to lay sick for months, with doctors' bills eatin' you up, and then have to go anyhow.

THIRD PALLBEARER

No; when a thing has to be done, the best thing to do is to get it done and over with.

FOURTH PALLBEARER

That's just what I said to my wife when I heerd.

FIFTH PALLBEARER

But nobody hardly thought that *he* woulda been the next.

FIRST PALLBEARER

No; but that's one of them things you can't tell.

FIRST PALLBEARER

You never know *who'll* be the next.

SECOND PALLBEARER

It's lucky you don't.

THIRD PALLBEARER

I guess you're right.

FOURTH PALLBEARER

That's what my grandfather used to say: you never know what is coming.

FIFTH PALLBEARER

Yes; that's the way it goes.

FIRST PALLBEARER

First one, and then somebody else.

FIRST PALLBEARER

Who it'll be you can't say.

SECOND PALLBEARER

I always say the same: we're here to-day — —

THIRD PALLBEARER

(*Cutting in jealousy and humorously.*) And to-morrow we ain't here.

(*A subdued and sinister snicker. It is followed by sudden silence. There is a shuffling of feet in the front room, and whispers. Necks are craned. The pallbearers straighten their backs, hitch their coat collars and pull on their black gloves. THE CLERGYMAN has arrived. From above comes the sound of weeping.*)

From The Programme of a Concert

"*Ruhm und Ewigkeit*" (*Fame and Eternity*), *a symphonic poem in B flat minor, Opus 48, by Johann Sigismund Timotheus Albert Wolfgang Kraus (1872-).*

Kraus, like his eminent compatriot, Dr. Richard Strauss, has gone to Friedrich Nietzsche, the laureate of the modern German tone-art, for his inspiration in this gigantic work. His text is to be found in Nietzsche's *Ecce Homo*, which was not published until after the poet's death, but the composition really belongs to *Also sprach Zarathustra*, as a glance will show:

I

Wie lange sitzest du schon
auf deinem Missgeschick?
Gieb Acht! Du brütest mir noch
ein Ei,
ein Basilisken-Ei,
aus deinem langen Jammer aus.

II

Was schleicht Zarathustra entlang dem Berge? —

III

Misstrauisch, geschwürig, düster,

ein langer Lauerer, —
aber plötzlich, ein Blitz,
hell, furchtbar, ein Schlag
gen Himmel aus dem Abgrund:
—dem Berge selber schüttelt sich
das Eingeweide....

IV

Wo Hass und Blitzstrahl
Eins ward, ein Fluch, —
auf den Bergen haust jetzt Zarathustra's Zorn,
eine Wetterwolke schleicht er seines Wegs.

V

Verkrieche sich, wer eine letzte Decke hat!
In's Bett mit euch, ihr Zärtlinge!
Nun rollen Donner über die Gewölbe,
nun zittert, was Gebälk und Mauer ist,
nun zucken Blitze und schwefelgelbe Wahrheiten —
Zarathustra flucht ...!

For the following faithful and graceful translation the present commentator is indebted to Mr. Louis Untermeyer:

I

How long brood you now
On thy disaster?
Give heed! You hatch me soon
An egg,
From your long lamentation out of.

II

Why prowls Zarathustra among the mountains?

III

Distrustful, ulcerated, dismal,
A long waiter—
But suddenly a flash, Brilliant, fearful.
A lightning stroke
Leaps to heaven from the abyss:
—The mountains shake themselves and
Their intestines....

IV

As hate and lightning-flash
Are united, a *curse!*
On the mountains rages now Zarathustra's wrath,
Like a thunder cloud rolls it on its way.

V

Crawl away, ye who have a roof remaining!
To bed with you, ye tenderlings!
Now thunder rolls over the great arches,
Now tremble the bastions and battlements,
Now flashes palpitate and sulphur-yellow truths—
Zarathustra swears ...!

The composition is scored for three flutes, one piccolo, one bass piccolo, seven oboes, one English horn, three clarinets in D flat, one clarinet in G flat, one corno de bassetto, three bassoons, one contra-bassoon, eleven horns, three trumpets, eight cornets in B, four trombones, two alto trombones, one viol da gamba, one mandolin, two guitars, one banjo, two tubas, glockenspiel, bell, triangle, fife, bass-drum, cymbals, timpani, celesta, four harps, piano, harmonium, pianola, phonograph, and the usual strings.

At the opening a long B flat is sounded by the cornets, clarinets and bassoons in unison, with soft strokes upon a kettle-drum tuned to G sharp. After eighteen measures of this, *singhiozzando*, the strings enter *pizzicato* with a figure based upon one of the scales of the ancient Persians—B flat, C flat, D, E sharp, G and A flat—which starts high among the first violins, and then proceeds downward, through the second violins, violas and cellos, until it is lost in solemn and indistinct mutterings in the double-basses. Then, the atmosphere of doom having been established, and the conductor having found his place in the score, there is heard the motive of brooding, or as the German commentators call it, the *Quälerei Motiv*:

The opening chord of the eleventh is sounded by six horns, and the chords of the ninth, which follow, are given to the woodwind. The rapid figure in the second measure is for solo violin, heard softly against the sustained interval of the diminished ninth, but the final G natural is snapped out by the whole orchestra *sforzando*. There follows a rapid and daring development of the theme, with the flutes and violoncellos leading, first harmonized with chords of the eleventh, then with chords of the thirteenth, and finally with chords of the fifteenth. Meanwhile, the tonality has moved into D minor, then into A flat major, and then into G sharp minor, and the little arpeggio for the solo violin has been augmented to seven, to eleven, and in the end to twenty-three notes. Here the influence of Claude Debussy shows itself; the chords of the ninth proceed by the same chromatic semitones that one finds in the *Chansons de Bilitis*. But Kraus goes much further than Debussy, for the tones of his chords are constantly altered in a strange and extremely beautiful manner, and, as has been noted, he adds the eleventh, thirteenth and fifteenth. At the end of this incomparable passage there is a sudden drop to C major, followed by the first statement of the *Missgeschick Motiv*, or motive of disaster (misfortune, evil destiny, untoward fate):

This graceful and ingratiating theme will give no concern to the student of Ravel and Schoenberg. It is, in fact, a quite elemental succession of intervals of the second, all produced by adding the ninth to the common chord—thus: C, G, C, D, E—with certain enharmonic changes. Its simplicity gives it, at a first hearing, a placid, pastoral aspect, somewhat disconcerting to the literalist, but the discerning will not fail to note the mutterings beneath the surface. It is first sounded by two violas and the viol da gamba, and then drops without change to the bass, where it is repeated *fortissimo* by two bassoons and the contra-bassoon. The tempo then quickens and the two themes so far heard are worked up into a brief but tempestuous fugue. A brief extract will suffice to show its enormously complex nature:

A pedal point on B flat is heard at the end of this fugue, sounded *fortissimo* by all the brass in unison, and then follows a grand pause, twelve and a half measures in length. Then, in the strings, is heard the motive of warning:

Out of this motive comes the harmonic material for much of what remains of the composition. At each repetition of the theme, the chord in the fourth measure is augmented by the addition of another interval, until in the end it includes every tone of the chromatic scale save C sharp. This omission is significant of Kraus' artistry. If C sharp were included the tonality would at once become vague, but without it the dependence of the whole gorgeous edifice upon C major is kept plain. At the end, indeed, the tonic chord of C major is clearly sounded by the wood-wind, against curious triplets, made up of F sharp, A flat and B flat in various combinations, in the strings; and from it a sudden modulation is made to C minor, and then to A flat major. This opens the way for the entrance of the motive of lamentation, or, as the German commentators call it, the *Schreierei Motiv*:

This simple and lovely theme is first sounded, not by any of the usual instruments of the grand orchestra, but by a phonograph in B flat, with the accompaniment of a solitary trombone. When the composition was first played at the Gewandhaus in Leipzig the innovation caused a sensation, and there were loud cries of sacrilege and even proposals of police action. One indignant classicist, in token of his ire, hung a wreath of *Knackwürste* around the neck of the bust of Johann Sebastian Bach in the Thomaskirche, and appended to it a card bearing the legend, *Schweinehund*! But the exquisite beauty of the effect soon won acceptance for the means employed to attain it, and the phonograph has so far made its way with German composers that Prof. Ludwig Grossetrommel, of Göttingen, has even proposed its employment in opera in place of singers.

This motive of lamentation is worked out on a grand scale, and in intimate association with the motives of brooding and of warning. Kraus is not content with the ordinary materials of composition. His creative force is always impelling him to break through the fetters of the diatonic scale, and to find utterance for his ideas in archaic and extremely exotic tonalities. The pentatonic scale is a favorite with him; he employs it as boldly as Wagner did in *Das Rheingold*. But it is not enough, for he proceeds from it into the Dorian mode of the ancient Greeks, and then into the Phrygian, and then into two of the plagal modes. Moreover, he constantly combines both unrelated scales and antagonistic motives, and invests the combinations in astounding orchestral colors, so that the hearer, unaccustomed to such bold experimentations, is quite lost in the maze. Here, for example, is a characteristic passage for solo French horn and bass piccolo:

The dotted half notes for the horn obviously come from the motive of brooding, in augmentation, but the bass piccolo part is new. It soon appears, however, in various fresh aspects, and in the end it enters into the famous quadruple motive of "sulphur-yellow truth"—*schwefelgelbe Wahrheit*, as we shall presently see. Its first combination is with a jaunty figure in A minor, and the two together form what most of the commentators agree upon denominating the Zarathustra motive:

I call this the Zarathustra motive, following the weight of critical opinion, but various influential critics dissent. Thus, Dr. Ferdinand Bierfisch, of the Hochschule für Musik at Dresden, insists that it is the theme of "the elevated mood produced by the spiritual isolation and low barometric pressure of the mountains," while Prof. B. Moll, of Frankfurt a/M., calls it the motive of prowling. Kraus himself, when asked by Dr. Fritz Bratsche, of the Berlin *Volkszeitung*, shrugged his shoulders and answered in his native Hamburg dialect, "*So gehts im Leben! 'S giebt gar kein Use*"—Such is life; it gives hardly any use (to inquire?). In much the same way Schubert made reply to one who asked the meaning of the opening subject of the slow movement of his C major symphony: "*Halt's Maul, du verfluchter Narr!*"—Don't ask such question, my dear sir!

But whatever the truth, the novelty and originality of the theme cannot be denied, for it is in two distinct keys, D major and A minor, and they preserve their identity whenever it appears. The handling of two such diverse tonalities at one time would present insuperable difficulties to a composer less ingenious than Kraus, but he manages it quite simply by founding his whole harmonic scheme upon the tonic triad of D major, with the seventh and ninth added. He thus achieves a chord which also contains the tonic triad of A minor. The same thing is now done with the dominant triads, and half the battle is won. Moreover, the instrumentation shows the same boldness, for the double theme is first given to three solo violins, and they are muted in a novel and effective manner by stopping their F holes. The directions in the score say *mit Glaserkitt* (that is, with glazier's putty), but the Konzertmeister at the Gewandhaus, Herr F. Dur, substituted ordinary pumpernickel with excellent results. It is, in fact, now commonly used in the German orchestras in place of putty, for it does less injury to the varnish of the violins, and, besides, it is edible after use. It produces a thick, oily, mysterious, far-away effect.

At the start, as I have just said, the double theme of Zarathustra appears in D major and A minor, but there is quick modulation to B flat major and C sharp minor, and then to C major and F sharp minor. Meanwhile the tempo gradually accelerates, and the polyphonic texture is helped out by reminiscences of the themes of brooding and of lamentation. A sudden hush and the motive of warning is heard high in the wood-wind, in C flat major, against a double organ-point—C natural and C sharp—in the lower strings. There follows a cadenza of no less than eighty-four measures for four harps, tympani and a single tuba, and then the motive of waiting is given out by the whole orchestra in unison:

19

This stately motive is repeated in F major, after which some passage work for the piano and pianola, the former tuned a quarter tone lower than the latter and played by three performers, leads directly into the quadruple theme of the sulphur-yellow truth, mentioned above. It is first given out by two oboes divided, a single English horn, two bassoons in unison, and four trombones in unison. It is an extraordinarily long motive, running to twenty-seven measures on its first appearance; the four opening measures are given on the next page.

With an exception yet to be noted, all of the composer's thematic material is now set forth, and what follows is a stupendous development of it, so complex that no written description could even faintly indicate its character. The quadruple theme of the sulphur-yellow truth is sung almost uninterruptedly, first by the wood-wind, then by the strings and then by the full brass choir, with the glockenspiel and cymbals added. Into it are woven all of the other themes in inextricable whirls and whorls of sound, and in most amazing combinations and permutations of tonalities. Moreover, there is a constantly rising complexity of rhythm, and on one page of the score the time signature is changed no less than eighteen times. Several times it is 5-8 and 7-4; once it is 11-2; in one place the composer, following Koechlin and Erik Satie, abandons bar-lines altogether for half a page of the score. And these diverse rhythms are not always merely successive; sometimes they are heard together. For example, the motive of disaster, augmented to 5-8 time, is sounded clearly by the clarinets against the motive of lamentation in 3-4 time, and through it all one hears the steady beat of the motive of waiting in 4-4!

This gigantic development of materials is carried to a thrilling climax, with the whole orchestra proclaiming the Zarathustra motive *fortissimo*. Then follows a series of arpeggios for the harps, made of the motive of warning, and out of them there gradually steals the tonic triad of D minor, sung by three oboes. This chord constitutes the backbone of all that follows. The three oboes are presently joined by a fourth. Against this curtain of tone the flutes and piccolos repeat the theme of brooding in F major, and then join the oboes in the D minor chord. The horns and bassoons follow with the motive of disaster and then do likewise. Now come the violins with the motive of lamentation, but instead of ending with

21

the D minor tonic triad, they sound a chord of the seventh erected on C sharp as seventh of D minor. Every tone of the scale of D minor is now being sounded, and as instrument after instrument joins in the effect is indescribably sonorous and imposing. Meanwhile, there is a steady *crescendo*, ending after three minutes of truly tremendous music with ten sharp blasts of the double chord. A moment of silence and a single trombone gives out a theme hitherto not heard. It is the theme of tenderness, or, as the German commentators call it, the *Biermad'l Motiv*: Thus:

Again silence. Then a single piccolo plays the closing cadence of the composition:

Ruhm und Ewigkeit presents enormous difficulties to the performers, and taxes the generalship of the most skillful conductor. When it was in preparation at the Gewandhaus the first performance was postponed twelve times in order to extend the rehearsals. It was reported in the German papers at the time that ten members of the orchestra, including the first flutist, Ewald Löwenhals, resigned during the rehearsals, and that the intervention of the King of Saxony was necessary to make them reconsider their resignations.

One of the second violins, Hugo Zehndaumen, resorted to stimulants in anticipation of the opening performance, and while on his way to the hall was run over by a taxicab. The conductor was Nikisch. A performance at Munich followed, and on May 1, 1913, the work reached Berlin. At the public rehearsal there was a riot led by members of the Bach Gesellschaft, and the hall was stormed by the mounted police. Many arrests were made, and five of the rioters were taken to hospital with serious injuries. The work was put into rehearsal by the Boston Symphony Orchestra in 1914. The rehearsals have been proceeding ever since. A piano transcription for sixteen hands has been published.

Kraus was born at Hamburg on January 14, 1872. At the age of three he performed creditably on the zither, cornet and trombone, and by 1877 he had already appeared in concert at Danzig. His family was very poor, and his early years were full of difficulties. It is said that, at the age of nine, he copied the whole score of Wagner's *Ring*, the scores of the nine Beethoven symphonies and the complete works of Mozart. His regular teacher, in those days, was Stadtpfeifer Schmidt, who instructed him in piano and thorough-bass. In 1884, desiring to have lessons in counterpoint from Prof. Kalbsbraten, of Mainz, he walked to that city from Hamburg once a week—a distance for the round trip of 316 miles. In 1887 he went to Berlin and became fourth cornetist of the Philharmonic Orchestra and valet to Dr. Schweinsrippen, the conductor. In Berlin he studied violin and second violin under the Polish virtuoso, Pbyschbrweski, and also had lessons in composition from Wilhelm Geigenheimer, formerly third triangle and assistant librarian at Bayreuth.

His first composition, a march for cornet, violin and piano, was performed on July 18, 1888, at the annual ball of the Arbeiter

Liedertafel in Berlin. It attracted little attention, but six months later the young composer made musical Berlin talk about him by producing a composition called *Adenoids*, for twelve tenors, *a cappella*, to words by Otto Julius Bierbaum. This was first heard at an open air concert given in the Tiergarten by the Sozialist Liederkranz. It was soon after repeated by the choir of the Gottesgelehrheitsakademie, and Kraus found himself a famous young man. His string quartet in G sharp minor, first played early in 1889 by the quartet led by Prof. Rudolph Wurst, added to his growing celebrity, and when his first tone poem for orchestra, *Fuchs, Du Hast die Gans Gestohlen*, was done by the Philharmonic in the autumn of 1889, under Dr. Lachschinken, it was hailed with acclaim.

Kraus has since written twelve symphonies (two choral), nine tone-poems, a suite for brass and tympani, a trio for harp, tuba and glockenspiel, ten string quartettes, a serenade for flute and contra-bassoon, four concert overtures, a cornet concerto, and many songs and piano pieces. His best-known work, perhaps, is his symphony in F flat major, in eight movements. But Kraus himself is said to regard this huge work as trivial. His own favorite, according to his biographer, Dr. Linsensuppe, is *Ruhm und Ewigkeit*, though he is also fond of the tone-poem which immediately preceded it, *Rinderbrust und Meerrettig*. He has written a choral for sixty trombones, dedicated to Field Marshal von Hindenburg, and is said to be at work on a military mass for four orchestras, seven brass bands and ten choirs, with the usual soloists and clergy. Among his principal works are *Der Ewigen Wiederkunft* (a ten part fugue for full orchestra), *Biergemütlichkeit*, his *Oberkellner* and *Uebermensch* concert overtures, and his setting (for mixed chorus) of the old German hymn:

Saufst—stirbst!
Saufst net—stirbst a!
Also, saufst!

Kraus is now a resident of Munich, where he conducts the orchestra at the Löwenbräuhaus. He has been married eight times and is at present the fifth husband of Tilly Heintz, the opera singer. He has been decorated by the Kaiser, by the King of Sweden and by the Sultan of Turkey, and is a member of the German Odd Fellows.

The Wedding. A Stage Direction

The scene is a church in an American city of about half a million population, and the time is about eleven o'clock of a fine morning in early spring. The neighborhood is well-to-do, but not quite fashionable. That is to say, most of the families of the vicinage keep two servants (alas, more or less intermittently!), and eat dinner at half-past six, and about one in every four boasts a colored butler (who attends to the fires, washes windows and helps with the sweeping), and a last year's automobile. The heads of these families are merchandise brokers; jobbers in notions, hardware and drugs; manufacturers of candy, hats, badges, office furniture, blank books, picture frames, wire goods and patent medicines; managers of steamboat lines; district agents of insurance companies; owners of commercial printing offices, and other such business men of substance—and the prosperous lawyers and popular family doctors who keep them out of trouble. In one block live a Congressman and two college professors, one of whom has written an unimportant textbook and got himself into "Who's Who in America." In the block above lives a man who once ran for Mayor of the city, and came near being elected.

The wives of these householders wear good clothes and have a liking for a reasonable gayety, but very few of them can pretend to what is vaguely called social standing, and, to do them justice, not many of them waste any time lamenting it. They have, taking one with another, about three children apiece, and are good mothers. A few of them belong to women's clubs or flirt with the suffragettes, but the majority can get all of the intellectual stimulation they crave in the Ladies' Home Journal and the

Saturday Evening Post, with Vogue added for its fashions. Most of them, deep down in their hearts, suspect their husbands of secret frivolity, and about ten per cent. have the proofs, but it is rare for them to make rows about it, and the divorce rate among them is thus very low. Themselves indifferent cooks, they are unable to teach their servants the art, and so the food they set before their husbands and children is often such as would make a Frenchman cut his throat. But they are diligent housewives otherwise; they see to it that the windows are washed, that no one tracks mud into the hall, that the servants do not waste coal, sugar, soap and gas, and that the family buttons are always sewed on. In religion these estimable wives are pious in habit but somewhat nebulous in faith. That is to say, they regard any person who specifically refuses to go to church as a heathen, but they themselves are by no means regular in attendance, and not one in ten of them could tell you whether transubstantiation is a Roman Catholic or a Dunkard doctrine. About two per cent. have dallied more or less gingerly with Christian Science, their average period of belief being one year.

The church we are in is like the neighborhood and its people: well-to-do but not fashionable. It is Protestant in faith and probably Episcopalian. The pews are of thick, yellow-brown oak, severe in pattern and hideous in color. In each there is a long, removable cushion of a dark, purplish, dirty hue, with here and there some of its hair stuffing showing. The stained-glass windows, which were all bought ready-made and depict scenes from the New Testament, commemorate the virtues of departed worthies of the neighborhood, whose names appear, in illegible black letters, in the lower panels. The floor is covered with a carpet of some tough, fibrous material, apparently a sort of grass, and along the center aisle it is much worn. The normal smell of the place is rather less unpleasant than that of most other halls, for on the one day when it is regularly crowded practically all of the persons gathered together have been very recently bathed.

27

On this fine morning, however, it is full of heavy, mortuary perfumes, for a couple of florist's men have just finished decorating the chancel with flowers and potted palms. Just behind the chancel rail, facing the center aisle, there is a prie-dieu, and to either side of it are great banks of lilies, carnations, gardenias and roses. Three or four feet behind the prie-dieu and completely concealing the high altar, there is a dense jungle of palms. Those in the front rank are authentically growing in pots, but behind them the florist's men have artfully placed some more durable, and hence more profitable, sophistications. Anon the rev. clergyman, emerging from the vestry-room to the right, will pass along the front of this jungle to the prie-dieu, and so, framed in flowers, face the congregation with his saponaceous smile.

The florist's men, having completed their labors, are preparing to depart. The older of the two, a man in the fifties, shows the ease of an experienced hand by taking out a large plug of tobacco and gnawing off a substantial chew. The desire to spit seizing him shortly, he proceeds to gratify it by a trick long practised by gasfitters, musicians, caterer's helpers, piano movers and other such alien invaders of the domestic hearth. That is to say, he hunts for a place where the carpet is loose along the chancel rail, finds it where two lengths join, deftly turns up a flap, spits upon the bare floor, and then lets the flap fall back, finally giving it a pat with the sole of his foot. This done, he and his assistant leave the church to the sexton, who has been sweeping the vestibule, and, after passing the time of day with the two men who are putting up a striped awning from the door to the curb, disappear into a nearby speak-easy, there to wait and refresh themselves until the wedding is over, and it is time to take away their lilies, their carnations and their synthetic palms.

It is now a quarter past eleven, and two flappers of the neighborhood, giggling and arm-in-arm, approach the sexton and inquire of him if they may enter. He asks them if they have tickets and when they say they

28

haven't, he tells them that he ain't got no right to let them in, and don't know nothing about what the rule is going to be. At some weddings, he goes on, hardly nobody ain't allowed in, but then again, sometimes they don't scarcely look at the tickets at all. The two flappers retire abashed, and as the sexton finishes his sweeping, there enters the organist.

The organist is a tall, thin man of melancholy, uræmic aspect, wearing a black slouch hat with a wide brim and a yellow overcoat that barely reaches to his knees. A pupil, in his youth, of a man who had once studied (irregularly and briefly) with Charles-Marie Widor, he acquired thereby the artistic temperament, and with it a vast fondness for malt liquor. His mood this morning is acidulous and depressed, for he spent yesterday evening in a Pilsner ausschank with two former members of the Boston Symphony Orchestra, and it was 3 A. M. before they finally agreed that Johann Sebastian Bach, all things considered, was a greater man than Beethoven, and so parted amicably. Sourness is the precise sensation that wells within him. He feels vinegary; his blood runs cold; he wishes he could immerse himself in bicarbonate of soda. But the call of his art is more potent than the protest of his poisoned and quaking liver, and so he manfully climbs the spiral stairway to his organ-loft.

Once there, he takes off his hat and overcoat, stoops down to blow the dust off the organ keys, throws the electrical switch which sets the bellows going, and then proceeds to take off his shoes. This done, he takes his seat, reaches for the pedals with his stockinged feet, tries an experimental 32-foot CCC, and then wanders gently into a Bach toccata. It is his limbering-up piece: he always plays it as a prelude to a wedding job. It thus goes very smoothly and even brilliantly, but when he comes to the end of it and tackles the ensuing fugue he is quickly in difficulties, and after four or five stumbling repetitions of the subject he hurriedly improvises a crude coda and has done. Peering down into the church to see if his flounderings have had an audience, he sees two old maids enter, the one very tall and thin and the other somewhat brisk and bunchy.

29

They constitute the vanguard of the nuptial throng, and as they proceed hesitatingly up the center aisle, eager for good seats but afraid to go too far, the organist wipes his palms upon his trousers legs, squares his shoulders, and plunges into the program that he has played at all weddings for fifteen years past. It begins with Mendelssohn's *Spring Song*, pianissimo. Then comes Rubinstein's *Melody in F*, with a touch of forte toward the close, and then Nevin's "Oh, That We Two Were Maying" and then the Chopin waltz in A flat, Opus 69, No. 1, and then the *Spring Song* again, and then a free fantasia upon "The Rosary" and then a Moszkowski mazurka, and then the Dvořák *Humoresque* (with its heart-rending cry in the middle), and then some vague and turbulent thing (apparently the disjecta membra of another fugue), and then Tschaikowsky's "Autumn," and then Elgar's "Salut d'Amour," and then the *Spring Song* a third time, and then something or other from one of the Peer Gynt suites, and then an hurrah or two from the Hallelujah chorus, and then Chopin again, and Nevin, and Elgar, and——

But meanwhile, there is a growing activity below. First comes a closed automobile bearing the six ushers and soon after it another automobile bearing THE BRIDEGROOM and his best man. THE BRIDEGROOM and the best man disembark before the side entrance of the church and make their way into the vestry room, where they remove their hats and coats, and proceed to struggle with their cravats and collars before a mirror which hangs on the wall. The room is very dingy. A baize-covered table is in the center of it, and around the table stand six or eight chairs of assorted designs. One wall is completely covered by a bookcase, through the glass doors of which one may discern piles of cheap Bibles, hymn-books and back numbers of the parish magazine. In one corner is a small washstand. The best man takes a flat flask of whiskey from his pocket, looks about him for a glass, finds it on the washstand, rinses it at the tap, fills it with a policeman's drink, and hands it to THE BRIDEGROOM. The latter downs it at a gulp. Then the best man pours out one for himself.

The ushers, reaching the vestibule of the church, have handed their silk hats to the sexton, and entered the sacred edifice. There was a rehearsal of the wedding last night, but after it was over the bride ordered certain incomprehensible changes in the plan, and the ushers are now completely at sea. All they know clearly is that the relatives of the bride are to be seated on one side and the relatives of THE BRIDEGROOM on the other. But which side for one and which for the other? They discuss it heatedly for three minutes and then find that they stand three for putting the bride's relatives on the left side and three for putting them on the right side. The debate, though instructive, is interrupted by the sudden entrance of seven women in a group. They are headed by a truculent old battleship, possibly an aunt or something of the sort, who fixes the nearest usher with a knowing, suspicious glance, and motions to him to show her the way.

He offers her his right arm and they start up the center aisle, with the six other women following in irregular order, and the five other ushers scattered among the women. The leading usher is tortured damnably by doubts as to where the party should go. If they are aunts, to which house do they belong, and on which side are the members of that house to be seated? What if they are not aunts, but merely neighbors? Or perhaps an association of former cooks, parlor maids, nurse girls? Or strangers? The sufferings of the usher are relieved by the battleship, who halts majestically about twenty feet from the altar, and motions her followers into a pew to the left. They file in silently and she seats herself next the aisle. All seven settle back and wriggle for room. It is a tight fit.

(Who, in point of fact, are these ladies? Don't ask the question! The ushers never find out. No one ever finds out. They remain a joint mystery for all time. In the end they become a sort of tradition, and years hence, when two of the ushers meet, they will cackle over old dreadnaught and her six cruisers. The bride, grown old and fat, will tell the tale to her daughter, and then to her granddaughter. It will grow more and more strange,

marvelous, incredible. Variorum versions will spring up. It will be adapted to other weddings. The dreadnaught will become an apparition, a witch, the Devil in skirts. And as the years pass, the date of the episode will be pushed back. By 2017 it will be dated 1150. By 2475 it will take on a sort of sacred character, and there will be a footnote referring to it in the latest Revised Version of the New Testament.)

It is now a quarter to twelve, and of a sudden the vestibule fills with wedding guests. Nine-tenths of them, perhaps even nineteen-twentieths, are women, and most of them are beyond thirty-five. Scattered among them, hanging on to their skirts, are about a dozen little girls—one of them a youngster of eight or thereabout, with spindle shanks and shining morning face, entranced by her first wedding. Here and there lurks a man. Usually he wears a hurried, unwilling, protesting look. He has been dragged from his office on a busy morning, forced to rush home and get into his cut-away coat, and then marched to the church by his wife. One of these men, much hustled, has forgotten to have his shoes shined. He is intensely conscious of them, and tries to hide them behind his wife's skirt as they walk up the aisle. Accidentally he steps upon it, and gets a look over the shoulder which lifts his diaphragm an inch and turns his liver to water. This man will be courtmartialed when he reaches home, and he knows it. He wishes that some foreign power would invade the United States and burn down all the churches in the country, and that the bride, THE BRIDEGROOM and all the other persons interested in the present wedding were dead and in hell.

The ushers do their best to seat these wedding guests in some sort of order, but after a few minutes the crowd at the doors becomes so large that they have to give it up, and thereafter all they can do is to hold out their right arms ingratiatingly and trust to luck. One of them steps on a fat woman's skirt, tearing it very badly, and she has to be helped back to the vestibule. There she seeks refuge in a corner, under a stairway leading up to the steeple, and essays to repair the damage with pins produced from various nooks and crevices of her person. Meanwhile the guilty usher stands in front of her, mumbling apologies and trying to look helpful. When she finishes her work and emerges from her improvised dry-dock, he again offers her his arm, but she sweeps past him without noticing him, and proceeds grandly to a seat far forward. She is a cousin to the bride's mother, and will make a report to every branch of the family that all six ushers disgraced the ceremony by appearing at it far gone in liquor.

Fifteen minutes are consumed by such episodes and divertisements. By the time the clock in the steeple strikes twelve the church is well filled. The music of the organist, who has now reached Mendelssohn's Spring Song for the third and last time, is accompanied by a huge buzz of whispers, and there is much craning of necks and long-distance nodding and smiling. Here and there an unusually gorgeous hat is the target of many converging glances, and of as many more or less satirical criticisms. To the damp funeral smell of the flowers at the altar, there has been added the cacodorous scents of forty or fifty different brands of talcum and rice powder. It begins to grow warm in the church, and a number of women open their vanity bags and duck down for stealthy dabs at their noses. Others, more reverent, suffer the agony of augmenting shines. One, a trickster, has concealed powder in her pocket handkerchief, and applies it dexterously while pretending to blow her nose.

THE BRIDEGROOM in the vestry-room, entering upon the second year (or is it the third?) of his long and ghastly wait, grows increasingly nervous, and when he hears the organist pass from the Spring Song into some more sonorous and stately thing he mistakes it for the wedding march from "Lohengrin," and is hot for marching upon the altar at once. The best man, an old hand, restrains him gently, and administers another sedative from the bottle. THE BRIDEGROOM's thoughts turn to gloomy things. He remembers sadly that he will never be able to laugh at benedicts

33

again; that his days of low, rabelaisian wit and care-free scoffing are over; that he is now the very thing he mocked so gaily but yesteryear. Like a drowning man, he passes his whole life in review—not, however, that part which is past, but that part which is to come. Odd fancies throng upon him. He wonders what his honeymoon will cost him, what there will be to drink at the wedding breakfast, what a certain girl in Chicago will say when she hears of his marriage. Will there be any children? He rather hopes not, for all those he knows appear so greasy and noisy, but he decides that he might conceivably compromise on a boy. But how is he going to make sure that it will not be a girl? The thing, as yet, is a medical impossibility—but medicine is making rapid strides. Why not wait until the secret is discovered? This sapient compromise pleases THE BRIDEGROOM, and he proceeds to a consideration of various problems of finance. And then, of a sudden, the organist swings unmistakably into "Lohengrin" and the best man grabs him by the arm.

There is now great excitement in the church. The bride's mother, two sisters, three brothers and three sisters-in-law have just marched up the center aisle and taken seats in the front pew, and all the women in the place are craning their necks toward the door. The usual electrical delay ensues. There is something the matter with the bride's train, and the two bridesmaids have a deuce of a time fixing it. Meanwhile THE BRIDE'S FATHER, in tight pantaloons and tighter gloves, fidgets and fumes in the vestibule, the six ushers crowd about him inanely, and the sexton rushes to and fro like a rat in a trap. Finally, all being ready, with the ushers formed two abreast, the sexton pushes a button, a small buzzer sounds in the organ loft, and the organist, as has been said, plunges magnificently into the fanfare of the "Lohengrin" march. Simultaneously the sexton opens the door at the bottom of the main aisle, and the wedding procession gets under weigh.

The bride and her father march first. Their step is so slow (about one beat *to two measures) that the father has some difficulty in maintaining his equilibrium, but the bride herself moves steadily and erectly, almost seeming to float. Her face is thickly encrusted with talcum in its various forms, so that she is almost a dead white. She keeps her eyelids lowered modestly, but is still acutely aware of every glance fastened upon her—not in the mass, but every glance individually. For example, she sees clearly, even through her eyelids, the still, cold smile of a girl in Pew 8 R—a girl who once made an unwomanly attempt upon THE BRIDEGROOM's affections, and was routed and put to flight by superior strategy. And her ears are open, too: she hears every "How sweet!" and "Oh, lovely!" and "Ain't she pale!" from the latitude of the last pew to the very glacis of the altar of God.*

While she has thus made her progress up the hymeneal chute, THE BRIDEGROOM and his best man have emerged from the vestryroom and begun the short march to the prie-dieu. They walk haltingly, clumsily, uncertainly, stealing occasional glances at the advancing bridal party. THE BRIDEGROOM feels of his lower right-hand waistcoat pocket; the ring is still there. The best man wriggles his cuffs. No one, however, pays any heed to them. They are not even seen, indeed, until the bride and her father reach the open space in front of the altar. There the bride and THE BRIDEGROOM find themselves standing side by side, but not a word is exchanged between them, nor even a look of recognition. They stand motionless, contemplating the ornate cushion at their feet, until THE BRIDE'S FATHER and the bridesmaids file to the left of the bride and the ushers, now wholly disorganized and imbecile, drape themselves in an irregular file along the altar rail. Then, the music having died down to a faint murmur and a hush having fallen upon the assemblage, they look up.

Before them, framed by foliage, stands the reverend gentleman of God who will presently link them in indissoluble chains—the estimable rector of the parish. He has got there just in time; it was, indeed, a close shave. But no

35

trace of haste or of anything else of a disturbing character is now visible upon his smooth, glistening, somewhat feverish face. That face is wholly occupied by his official smile, a thing of oil and honey all compact, a balmy, unctuous illumination—the secret of his success in life. Slowly his cheeks puff out, gleaming like soap-bubbles. Slowly he lifts his prayer-book from the prie-dieu and holds it droopingly. Slowly his soft caressing eyes engage it. There is an almost imperceptible stiffening of his frame. His mouth opens with a faint click. He begins to read.

The Ceremony of Marriage has begun.

IV

The Visionary

"Yes," said Cheops, helping his guest over a ticklish place, "I daresay this pile of rocks will last. It has cost me a pretty penny, believe me. I made up my mind at the start that it would be built of honest stone, or not at all. No cheap and shoddy brickwork for *me*! Look at Babylon. It's all brick, and it's always tumbling down. My ambassador there tells me that it costs a million a year to keep up the walls alone—mind you, the walls alone! What must it cost to keep up the palace, with all that fancy work!

"Yes, I grant you that brickwork *looks* good. But what of it? So does a cheap cotton night-shirt—you know the gaudy things those Theban peddlers sell to my sand-hogs down on the river bank. But does it *last*? Of course it doesn't. Well, I am putting up this pyramid to *stay* put, and I don't give a damn for its looks. I hear all sorts of funny cracks about it. My barber is a sharp nigger and keeps his ears open: he brings me all the gossip. But I let it go. This is *my* pyramid. I am putting up the money for it, and I have got to be mortared up in it when I die. So I am trying to make a good, substantial job of it, and letting the mere beauty of it go hang.

"Anyhow, there are plenty of uglier things in Egypt. Look at some of those fifth-rate pyramids up the river. When it comes to shape they are pretty much the same as this one, and when it comes to size, they look like warts beside it. And look at the Sphinx. There is something that cost four millions if it cost a copper—and what is it

37

now? A burlesque! A caricature! An architectural cripple! So long as it was *new*, good enough! It was a showy piece of work. People came all the way from Sicyonia and Tyre to gape at it. Everybody said it was one of the sights no one could afford to miss. But by and by a piece began to peel off here and another piece there, and then the nose cracked, and then an ear dropped off, and then one of the eyes began to get mushy and watery looking, and finally it was a mere smudge, a false-face, a scarecrow. My father spent a lot of money trying to fix it up, but what good did it do? By the time he had the nose cobbled the ears were loose again, and so on. In the end he gave it up as a bad job.

"Yes; this pyramid has kept me on the jump, but I'm going to stick to it if it breaks me. Some say I ought to have built it across the river, where the quarries are. Such gabble makes me sick. Do I look like a man who would go looking around for such *child's-play*? I hope not. A one-legged man could have done *that*. Even a Babylonian could have done it. It would have been as easy as milking a cow. What *I* wanted was something that would keep me on the jump—something that would put a strain on me. So I decided to haul the whole business *across* the river—six million tons of rock. And when the engineers said that it couldn't be done, I gave them two days to get out of Egypt, and then tackled it myself. It was something new and hard. It was a job I could get my teeth into.

"Well, I suppose you know what a time I had of it at the start. First I tried a pontoon bridge, but the stones for the bottom course were so heavy that they sank the pontoons, and I lost a couple of hundred niggers before I saw that it couldn't be done. Then I tried a big raft, but in order to get her to float with the stones I had to use such big logs that she was unwieldy, and before I knew what had struck me

I had lost six big dressed stones and another hundred niggers. I got the laugh, of course. Every numskull in Egypt wagged his beard over it; I could hear the chatter myself. But I kept quiet and stuck to the problem, and by and by I solved it.

"I suppose you know how I did it. In a general way? Well, the details are simple. First I made a new raft, a good deal lighter than the old one, and then I got a thousand water-tight goat-skins and had them blown up until they were as tight as drums. Then I got together a thousand niggers who were good swimmers, and gave each of them one of the blown-up goat-skins. On each goat-skin there was a leather thong, and on the bottom of the raft, spread over it evenly, there were a thousand hooks. Do you get the idea? Yes; that's it exactly. The niggers dived overboard with the goat-skins, swam under the raft, and tied the thongs to the hooks. And when all of them were tied on, the raft floated like a bladder. You simply *couldn't* sink it.

"Naturally enough, the thing took time, and there were accidents and setbacks. For instance, some of the niggers were so light in weight that they couldn't hold their goat-skins under water long enough to get them under the raft. I had to weight those fellows by having rocks tied around their middles. And when they had fastened their goat-skins and tried to swim back, some of them were carried down by the rocks. I never made any exact count, but I suppose that two or three hundred of them were drowned in that way. Besides, a couple of hundred were drowned because they couldn't hold their breaths long enough to swim under the raft and back. But what of it? I wasn't trying to hoard up niggers, but to make a raft that would float. And I did it.

"Well, once I showed how it could be done, all the wiseacres caught the idea, and after that I put a big gang to work making more rafts, and by and by I had sixteen of them in operation, and was hauling more stone than the masons could set. But I won't go into all that. Here is the pyramid; it speaks for itself. One year more and I'll have the top course laid and begin on the surfacing. I am going to make it plain marble, with no fancy work. I could bring in a gang of Theban stonecutters and have it carved all over with lions' heads and tiger claws and all that sort of gim-crackery, but why waste time and money? This isn't a menagerie, but a pyramid. My idea was to make it the boss pyramid of the world. The king who tries to beat it will have to get up pretty early in the morning.

"But what troubles I have had! Believe me, there has been nothing but trouble, trouble, trouble from the start. I set aside the engineering difficulties. They were hard for the engineers, but easy for me, once I put my mind on them. But the way these niggers have carried on has been something terrible. At the beginning I had only a thousand or two, and they all came from one tribe; so they got along fairly well. During the whole first year I doubt that more than twenty or thirty were killed in fights. But then I began to get fresh batches from up the river, and after that it was nothing but one fight after another. For two weeks running not a stroke of work was done. I really thought, at one time, that I'd have to give up. But finally the army put down the row, and after a couple of hundred of the ringleaders had been thrown into the river peace was restored. But it cost me, first and last, fully three thousand niggers, and set me back at least six months.

"Then came the so-called labor unions, and the strikes, and more trouble. These labor unions were started by a couple of smart, yellow niggers from Chaldea, one of them a sort of lay preacher, a fellow with a lot of gab. Before I got wind of them, they had gone so far it was almost impossible to squelch them. First I tried

40

conciliation, but it didn't work a bit. They made the craziest demands you ever heard of—a holiday every six days, meat every day, no night work and regular houses to live in. Some of them even had the effrontery to ask for money! Think of it! Niggers asking for money! Finally, I had to order out the army again and let some blood. But every time one was knocked over, I had to get another one to take his place, and that meant sending the army up the river, and more expense, and more devilish worry and nuisance.

"In my grandfather's time niggers were honest and faithful workmen. You could take one fresh from the bush, teach him to handle a shovel or pull a rope in a year or so, and after that he was worth almost as much as he could eat. But the nigger of to-day isn't worth a damn. He never does an honest day's work if he can help it, and he is forever wanting something. Take these fellows I have now—mainly young bucks from around the First Cataract. Here are niggers who never saw baker's bread or butcher's meat until my men grabbed them. They lived there in the bush like so many hyenas. They were ten days' march from a lemon. Well, now they get first-class beef twice a week, good bread and all the fish they can catch. They don't have to begin work until broad daylight, and they lay off at dark. There is hardly one of them that hasn't got a psaltery, or a harp, or some other musical instrument. If they want to dress up and make believe they are Egyptians, I give them clothes. If one of them is killed on the work, or by a stray lion, or in a fight, I have him embalmed by my own embalmers and plant him like a man. If one of them breaks a leg or loses an arm or gets too old to work, I turn him loose without complaining, and he is free to go home if he wants to.

"But are they contented? Do they show any gratitude? Not at all.

41

Scarcely a day passes that I don't hear of some fresh soldiering. And, what is worse, they have stirred up some of my own people — the carpenters, stone-cutters, gang bosses and so on. Every now and then my inspectors find some rotten libel cut on a stone — something to the effect that I am overworking them, and knocking them about, and holding them against their will, and generally mistreating them. I haven't the slightest doubt that some of these inscriptions have actually gone into the pyramid: it's impossible to watch every stone. Well, in the years to come, they will be dug out and read by strangers, and I will get a black eye. People will think of Cheops as a heartless old rapscallion — *me*, mind you! Can you beat it?"

V

The Artist. A Drama Without Words

Characters:

A Great Pianist
A Janitor
Six Musical Critics
A Married Woman
A Virgin
Sixteen Hundred and Forty-three Other Women
Six Other Men

Place—*A City of the United States.*

Time—*A December afternoon.*

(*During the action of the play not a word is uttered aloud. All of the speeches of the characters are supposed to be unspoken meditations only.*)

A large, gloomy hall, with many rows of uncushioned, uncomfortable seats, designed, it would seem, by some one misinformed as to the average width of the normal human pelvis. A number of busts of celebrated composers, once white, but now a dirty gray, stand in niches along the walls. At one end of the hall there is a bare, uncarpeted stage, with nothing on it save a grand piano and a chair. It is raining outside, and, as hundreds of people come crowding in, the air is laden with the mingled scents of umbrellas, raincoats, goloshes, cosmetics, perfumery and wet hair.

At eight minutes past four, The Janitor, after smoothing his hair with his hands and putting on a pair of detachable cuffs, emerges from the wings and crosses the stage, his shoes squeaking hideously at each step. Arriving at the piano, he opens it with solemn slowness. The job seems so absurdly trivial, even to so mean an understanding, that he can't refrain from glorifying it with a bit of hocus-pocus. This takes the form of a careful adjustment of a mysterious something within the instrument. He reaches in, pauses a moment as if in doubt, reaches in again, and then permits a faint smile of conscious sapience and efficiency to illuminate his face. All of this accomplished, he tiptoes back to the wings, his shoes again squeaking.

THE JANITOR

Now all of them people think I'm the professor's tuner. (*The thought gives him such delight that, for the moment, his brain is numbed. Then he proceeds.*) I guess them tuners make pretty good money. I wish I could get the hang of the trick. It *looks* easy. (*By this time he has disappeared in the wings and the stage is again a desert. Two or three women, far back in the hall, start a halfhearted handclapping. It dies out at once. The noise of rustling programs and shuffling feet succeeds it.*)

FOUR HUNDRED OF THE WOMEN

Oh, I do *certainly* hope he plays that lovely *Valse Poupée* as an encore! They say he does it better than Bloomfield-Zeisler.

ONE OF THE CRITICS

I hope the animal doesn't pull any encore numbers that I don't recognize. All of these people will buy the paper to-morrow morning just to find out what they have heard. It's infernally embarrassing to have to ask the manager. The public expects a musical critic to be a sort of walking thematic catalogue. The public is an ass.

THE SIX OTHER MEN

Oh, Lord! What a way to spend an afternoon!

A HUNDRED OF THE WOMEN

I wonder if he's as handsome as Paderewski.

ANOTHER HUNDRED OF THE WOMEN

I wonder if he's as gentlemanly as Josef Hofmann.

STILL ANOTHER HUNDRED WOMEN

I wonder if he's as fascinating as De Pachmann.

YET OTHER HUNDREDS

I wonder if he has dark eyes. You never can tell by those awful photographs in the newspapers.

HALF A DOZEN WOMEN

I wonder if he can really play the piano.

THE CRITIC AFORESAID

What a hell of a wait! These rotten piano-thumping immigrants deserve a hard call-down. But what's the use? The piano manufacturers bring them over here to wallop their pianos—and the piano manufacturers are not afraid to advertise. If you knock them too hard you have a nasty business-office row on your hands.

ONE OF THE MEN

If they allowed smoking, it wouldn't be so bad.

ANOTHER MAN

I wonder if that woman across the aisle— —

(*The Great Pianist bounces upon the stage so suddenly that he is bowing in the center before any one thinks to applaud. He makes three stiff bows. At the second the applause begins, swelling at once to a roar. He steps up to the piano, bows three times more, and then sits down. He hunches his shoulders, reaches for the pedals with his feet, spreads out his hands and waits for the clapper-clawing to cease. He is an undersized, paunchy East German, with hair the color of wet hay, and an extremely pallid complexion. Talcum powder hides the fact that his nose is shiny and somewhat pink. His eyebrows are carefully penciled and there are artificial shadows under his eyes. His face is absolutely expressionless.*)

THE VIRGIN

Oh!

THE MARRIED WOMEN

Oh!

THE OTHER WOMEN

Oh! How dreadfully handsome!

THE VIRGIN

Oh, such eyes, such depth! How he must have suffered! I'd like to hear him play the Prélude in D flat major. It would drive you crazy!

A HUNDRED OTHER WOMEN

I certainly *do* hope he plays some Schumann.

OTHER WOMEN

What beautiful hands! I could kiss them!

(The Great Pianist, *throwing back his head, strikes the massive opening chords of a Beethoven sonata. There is a sudden hush and each note is heard clearly. The tempo of the first movement, which begins after a grand pause, is* allegro con brio, *and the first subject is given out in a sparkling cascade of sound. But, despite the buoyancy of the music, there is an unmistakable undercurrent of melancholy in the playing. The audience doesn't fail to notice it.*)

THE VIRGIN

Oh, perfect! I could love him! Paderewski played it like a fox trot. What poetry *he* puts into it! I can see a soldier lover marching off to war.

ONE OF THE CRITICS

The ass is dragging it. Doesn't *con brio* mean—well, what the devil *does* it mean? I forget. I must look it up before I write the notice. Somehow, *brio* suggests cheese. Anyhow, Pachmann plays it a damn sight faster. It's safe to say *that*, at all events.

THE MARRIED WOMAN

Oh, I could listen to that sonata all day! The poetry he puts into it— even into the *allegro*! Just think what the *andante* will be! I like music to be sad.

ANOTHER WOMAN

What a sob he gets into it!

MANY OTHER WOMEN

How exquisite!

THE GREAT PIANIST

(*Gathering himself together for the difficult development section.*) That

47

American beer will be the death of me! I wonder what they put in it to give it its gassy taste. And the so-called German beer they sell over here—*du heiliger Herr Jesu!* Even Bremen would be ashamed of it. In München the police would take a hand.

(*Aiming for the first and second C's above the staff, he accidentally strikes the C sharps instead and has to transpose three measures to get back into the key. The effect is harrowing, and he gives his audience a swift glance of apprehension.*)

TWO HUNDRED AND FIFTY WOMEN

What new beauties he gets out of it!

A MAN

He can tickle the ivories, all right, all right!

A CRITIC

Well, at any rate, he doesn't try to imitate Paderewski.

THE GREAT PIANIST

(*Relieved by the non-appearance of the hisses he expected.*) Well, it's lucky for me that I'm not in Leipzig to-day! But in Leipzig an artist runs no risks: the beer is pure. The authorities see to that. The worse enemy of technic is biliousness, and biliousness is sure to follow bad beer. (*He gets to the coda at last and takes it at a somewhat livelier pace.*)

THE VIRGIN

How I envy the woman he loves! How it would thrill me to feel his arms about me—to be drawn closer, closer, closer! I would give up the whole world! What are conventions, prejudices, legal forms,

morality, after all? Vanities! Love is beyond and above them all—
and art is love! I think I must be a pagan.

THE GREAT PIANIST

And the herring! Good God, what herring! These barbarous
Americans— —

THE VIRGIN

Really, I am quite indecent! I should blush, I suppose. But love is
never ashamed—How people misunderstand me!

THE MARRIED WOMAN

I wonder if he's faithful. The chances are against it. I never heard of
a man who was. (*An agreeable melancholy overcomes her and she gives
herself up to the mood without thought.*)

THE GREAT PIANIST

I wonder whatever became of that girl in Dresden. Every time I
think of her, she suggests pleasant thoughts—good beer, a fine
band, *Gemütlichkeit*. I must have been in love with her—not much,
of course, but just enough to make things pleasant. And not a single
letter from her! I suppose she thinks I'm starving to death over
here—or tuning pianos. Well, when I get back with the money
there'll be a shock for her. A shock—but not a *Pfennig*!

THE MARRIED WOMAN

(*Her emotional coma ended.*) Still, you can hardly blame him. There
must be a good deal of temptation for a great artist. All of these
frumps here would— —

THE VIRGIN

Ah, how dolorous, how exquisite is love! How small the world would seem if— —

THE MARRIED WOMAN

Of course you could hardly call such old scarecrows temptations. But still— —

(*The Great Pianist comes to the last measure of the* coda—*a passage of almost Haydnesque clarity and spirit. As he strikes the broad chord of the tonic there comes a roar of applause. He arises, moves a step or two down the stage, and makes a series of low bows, his hands to his heart.*)

THE GREAT PIANIST

(*Bowing.*) I wonder why the American women always wear raincoats to piano recitals. Even when the sun is shining brightly, one sees hundreds of them. What a disagreeable smell they give to the hall. (*More applause and more bows.*) An American audience always smells of rubber and lilies-of-the-valley. How different in London! There an audience always smells of soap. In Paris it reminds you of sachet bags—and *lingerie.*

(*The applause ceases and he returns to the piano.*)

And now comes that *verfluchte adagio.*

(*As he begins to play, a deathlike silence falls upon the hall.*)

ONE OF THE CRITICS

What rotten pedaling!

ANOTHER CRITIC

A touch like a xylophone player, but he knows how to use his feet.

That suggests a good line for the notice—"he plays better with his feet than with his hands," or something like that. I'll have to think it over and polish it up.

ONE OF THE OTHER MEN

Now comes some more of that awful classical stuff.

THE VIRGIN

Suppose he can't speak English? But that wouldn't matter. Nothing matters. Love is beyond and above——

SIX HUNDRED WOMEN

Oh, how beautiful!

THE MARRIED WOMAN

Perfect!

THE DEAN OF THE CRITICS

(*Sinking quickly into the slumber which always overtakes him during the adagio.*) C-c-c-c-c-c-c-c-c-h-h-h-h-h-h-h-h!

THE YOUNGEST CRITIC

There is that old fraud asleep again. And to-morrow he'll print half a column of vapid reminiscence and call it criticism. It's a wonder his paper stands for him. Because he once heard Liszt, he....

THE GREAT PIANIST

That plump girl over there on the left is not so bad. As for the rest, I beg to be excused. The American women have no more shape than so many matches. They are too tall and too thin. I like a nice

51

rubbery armful—like that Dresden girl. Or that harpist in Moscow—the girl with the Pilsner hair. Let me see, what was her name? Oh, Fritzi, to be sure—but her last name? Schmidt? Kraus? Meyer? I'll have to try to think of it, and send her a postcard.

THE MARRIED WOMAN

What delicious flutelike tones!

ONE OF THE WOMEN

If Beethoven could only be here to hear it! He would cry for very joy! Maybe he *does* hear it. Who knows? I believe he does. I am *sure* he does.

(The Great Pianist *reaches the end of the* adagio, *and there is another burst of applause, which awakens* The Dean of the Critics.)

THE DEAN OF THE CRITICS

Oh, piffle! Compared to Gottschalk, the man is an amateur. Let him go back to the conservatory for a couple of years.

ONE OF THE MEN

(*Looking at his program.*) Next comes the *shirt-so*. I hope it has some tune in it.

THE VIRGIN

The *adagio* is love's agony, but the *scherzo* is love triumphant. What beautiful eyes he has! And how pale he is!

THE GREAT PIANIST

(*Resuming his grim toil.*) Well, there's half of it over. But this *scherzo* is ticklish business. That horrible evening in Prague—will I ever forget it? Those hisses—and the papers next day!

ONE OF THE MEN

Go it, professor! That's the best you've done yet!

ONE OF THE CRITICS

Too fast!

ANOTHER CRITIC

Too slow!

A YOUNG GIRL

My, but ain't the professor just full of talent!

THE GREAT PIANIST

Well, so far no accident. (*He negotiates a difficult passage, and plays it triumphantly, but at some expenditure of cold perspiration.*) What a way for a man to make a living!

THE VIRGIN

What passion he puts into it! His soul is in his finger-tips.

A CRITIC

A human pianola!

THE GREAT PIANIST

This *scherzo* always fetches the women. I can hear them draw long breaths. That plump girl is getting pale. Well, why shouldn't she? I suppose I'm about the best pianist she has ever heard—or ever *will* hear. What people can see in that Hambourg fellow I never could imagine. In Chopin, Schumann, Grieg, you might fairly say he's pretty good. But it takes an *artist* to play Beethoven. (*He rattles on to the end of the* scherzo *and there is more applause. Then he dashes into the* finale.)

THE DEAN OF THE CRITICS

Too loud! Too loud! It sounds like an ash-cart going down an alley. But what can you expect? Piano-playing is a lost art. Paderewski ruined it.

THE GREAT PIANIST

I ought to clear 200,000 marks by this tournee. If it weren't for those thieving agents and hotelkeepers, I'd make 300,000. Just think of it—twenty-four marks a day for a room! That's the way these Americans treat a visiting artist! The country is worse than Bulgaria. I was treated better at Bucharest. Well, it won't last forever. As soon as I get enough of their money they'll see me no more. Vienna is the place to settle down. A nice studio at fifty marks a month—and the life of a gentleman. What was the name of that little red-cheeked girl at the café in the Franzjosefstrasse—that girl with the gold tooth and the silk stockings? I'll have to look her up.

THE VIRGIN

What an artist! What a master! What a— —

THE MARRIED WOMAN

Has he really suffered, or is it just intuition?

THE GREAT PIANIST

No, marriage is a waste of money. Let the other fellow marry her.

(He approaches the closing measures of the finale.) And now for a breathing spell and a swallow of beer. American beer! Bah! But it's better than nothing. The Americans drink water. Cattle! Animals! *Ach, München, wie bist du so schön!*

(As he concludes there is a whirlwind of applause and he is forced to bow again and again. Finally, he is permitted to retire, and the audience prepares to spend the short intermission in whispering, grunting, wriggling, scraping its feet, rustling its programs and gaping at hats. The Six Musical Critics *and* Six Other Men, *their lips parched and their eyes staring, gallop for the door. As* The Great Pianist *comes from the stage,* The Janitor *meets him with a large seidel of beer. He seizes it eagerly and downs it at a gulp.)*

THE JANITOR

My, but them professors can put the stuff away!

VI

Seeing The World

The scene is the brow of the Hungerberg at Innsbruck. It is the half hour before sunset, and the whole lovely valley of the Inn—still wie die Nacht, tief wie das Meer—begins to glow with mauves and apple greens, apricots and silvery blues. Along the peaks of the great snowy mountains which shut it in, as if from the folly and misery of the world, there are touches of piercing primary colours—red, yellow, violet. Far below, hugging the winding river, lies little Innsbruck, with its checkerboard parks and Christmas garden villas. A battalion of Austrian soldiers, drilling in the Exerzierplatz, appears as an army of grey ants, now barely visible. Somewhere to the left, beyond the broad flank of the Hungerberg, the night train for Venice labours toward the town.

It is a superbly beautiful scene, perhaps the most beautiful in all Europe. It has colour, dignity, repose. The Alps here come down a bit and so increase their spell. They are not the harsh precipices of Switzerland, nor the too charming stage mountains of the Trentino, but rotting billows of clouds and snow, the high flung waves of some titanic but stricken ocean. Now and then comes a faint clank of metal from the funicular railway, but the tracks themselves are hidden among the trees of the lower slopes. The tinkle of an angelus bell (or maybe it is only a sheep bell) is heard from afar. A great bird, an eagle or a falcon, sweeps across the crystal spaces.

Here where we are is a shelf on the mountainside, and the hand of man has converted it into a terrace. To the rear, clinging to the mountain, is an Alpine gasthaus—a bit overdone, perhaps, with its red-framed windows and elaborate fretwork, but still genuinely of the Alps. Along the front of the terrace, protecting sightseers from the sheer drop of a thousand feet, is a stout wooden rail.

A man in an American sack suit, with a bowler hat on his head, lounges against this rail. His elbows rest upon it, his legs are crossed in the fashion of a figure four, and his face is buried in the red book of Herr Baedeker. It is the volume on Southern Germany, and he is reading the list of Munich hotels. Now and then he stops to mark one with a pencil, which he wets at his lips each time. While he is thus engaged, another man comes ambling along the terrace, apparently from the direction of the funicular railway station. He, too, carries a red book. It is Baedeker on Austria-Hungary. After gaping around him a bit, this second man approaches the rail near the other and leans his elbows upon it. Presently he takes a package of chewing gum from his coat pocket, selects two pieces, puts them into his mouth and begins to chew. Then he spits idly into space, idly but homerically, a truly stupendous expectoration, a staggering discharge from the Alps to the first shelf of the Lombard plain! THE FIRST MAN, startled by the report, glances up. Their eyes meet and there is a vague glimmer of recognition.

THE FIRST MAN

American?

THE SECOND MAN

Yes; St. Louis.

THE FIRST MAN

Been over long?

THE SECOND MAN

A couple of months.

THE FIRST MAN

What ship'd you come over in?

THE SECOND MAN

The *Kronprinz Friedrich*.

THE FIRST MAN

Aha, the German line! I guess you found the grub all right.

THE SECOND MAN

Oh, in the main. I have eaten better, but then again, I have eaten worse.

THE FIRST MAN

Well, they charge you enough for it, whether you get it or not. A man could live at the Plaza cheaper.

THE SECOND MAN

I should *say* he could. What boat did *you* come over in?

THE FIRST MAN

The *Maurentic*.

THE SECOND MAN

How is she?

THE FIRST MAN

Oh, so-so.

58

THE SECOND MAN

I hear the meals on those English ships are nothing to what they used to be.

THE FIRST MAN

That's what everybody tells me. But, as for me, I can't say I found them so bad. I had to send back the potatoes twice and the breakfast bacon once, but they had very good lima beans.

THE SECOND MAN

Isn't that English bacon awful stuff to get down?

THE FIRST MAN

It certainly is: all meat and gristle. I wonder what an Englishman would say if you put him next to a plate of genuine, crisp, *American* bacon.

THE SECOND MAN

I guess he would yell for the police—or choke to death.

THE FIRST MAN

Did you like the German cooking on the *Kronprinz*?

THE SECOND MAN

Well, I did and I didn't. The chicken à la Maryland was very good, but they had it only once. I could eat it every day.

THE FIRST MAN

Why didn't you order it?

59

THE SECOND MAN

It wasn't on the bill.

THE FIRST MAN

Oh, bill be damned! You might have ordered it anyhow. Make a fuss and you'll get what you want. These foreigners have to be bossed around. They're used to it.

THE SECOND MAN

I guess you're right. There was a fellow near me who set up a holler about his room the minute he saw it—said it was dark and musty and not fit to pen a hog in—and they gave him one twice as large, and the chief steward bowed and scraped to him, and the room stewards danced around him as if he was a duke. And yet I heard later that he was nothing but a Bismarck herring importer from Hoboken.

THE FIRST MAN

Yes, that's the way to get what you want. Did you have any nobility on board?

THE SECOND MAN

Yes, there was a Hungarian baron in the automobile business, and two English sirs. The baron was quite a decent fellow: I had a talk with him in the smoking room one night. He didn't put on any airs at all. You would have thought he was an ordinary man. But the sirs kept to themselves. All they did the whole voyage was to write letters, wear their dress suits and curse the stewards.

THE FIRST MAN

They tell me over here that the best eating is on the French lines.

THE SECOND MAN

Yes, so I hear. But some say, too, that the Scandinavian lines are best, and then again I have heard people boosting the Italian lines.

THE FIRST MAN

I guess each one has its points. They say that you get wine free with meals on the French boats.

THE SECOND MAN

But I hear it's fourth-rate wine.

THE FIRST MAN

Well, you don't have to drink it.

THE SECOND MAN

That's so. But, as for me, I can't stand a Frenchman. I'd rather do without the wine and travel with the Dutch. Paris is dead compared with Berlin.

THE FIRST MAN

So it is. But those Germans are awful sharks. The way they charge in Berlin is enough to make you sick.

THE SECOND MAN

Don't tell *me*. I have been there. No longer ago than last Tuesday— or was it last Monday?—I went into one of those big restaurants on the Unter den Linden and ordered a small steak, French fried potatoes, a piece of pie and a cup of coffee—and what do you think those thieves charged me for it? Three marks fifty. That's eighty-seven and a half cents. Why, a man could have got the same meal at home for a dollar. These Germans are running wild. American money has gone to their heads. They think every American they get hold of is a millionaire.

THE FIRST MAN

The French are worse. I went into a hotel in Paris and paid ten francs a day for a room for myself and wife, and when we left they charged me one franc forty a day extra for sweeping it out and making the bed!

THE SECOND MAN

That's nothing. Here in Innsbruck they charge you half a krone a day *taxes*.

THE FIRST MAN

What! You don't say!

THE SECOND MAN

Sure thing. And if you don't eat breakfast in the hotel they charge you a krone for it anyhow.

THE FIRST MAN

Well, well, what next? But, after all, you can't blame them. We Americans come over here and hand them our pocket-books, and we ought to be glad if we get anything back at all. The way a man has to tip is something fearful.

THE SECOND MAN

Isn't it, though! I stayed in Dresden a week, and when I left there were six grafters lined up with their claws out. First came the port*eer*. Then came— —

THE FIRST MAN

How much did you give the por*teer*?

THE SECOND MAN

Five marks.

THE FIRST MAN

You gave him too much. You ought to have given him about three marks, or, say, two marks fifty. How much was your hotel bill?

THE SECOND MAN

Including everything?

THE FIRST MAN

No, just your bill for your room.

THE SECOND MAN

I paid six marks a day.

THE FIRST MAN

Well, that made forty-two marks for the week. Now the way to figure out how much the por*teer* ought to get is easy: a fellow I met in Baden-Baden showed me how to do it. First, you multiply your hotel bill by two, then you divide it by twenty-seven, and then you knock off half a mark. Twice forty-two is eighty-four. Twenty-seven into eighty-four goes about three times, and half from three leaves two and a half. See how easy it is?

THE SECOND MAN

It *looks* easy, anyhow. But you haven't got much time to do all that figuring.

THE FIRST MAN

Well, let the port*eer* wait. The longer he has to wait the more he appreciates you.

THE SECOND MAN

But how about the others?

THE FIRST MAN

It's just as simple. Your chambermaid gets a quarter of a mark for every day you have been in the hotel. But if you stay less than four days she gets a whole mark anyhow. If there are two in the party she gets half a mark a day, but no more than three marks in any one week.

THE SECOND MAN

But suppose there are two chambermaids? In Dresden there was one on day duty and one on night duty. I left at six o'clock in the evening, and so they were both on the job.

THE FIRST MAN

Don't worry. They'd have been on the job anyhow, no matter when you left. But it's just as easy to figure out the tip for two as for one. All you have to do is to add fifty per cent. and then divide it into two halves, and give one to each girl. Or, better still, give it all to one girl and tell her to give half to her pal. If there are three chambermaids, as you sometimes find in the swell hotels, you add another fifty per cent. and then divide by three. And so on.

THE SECOND MAN

I see. But how about the hall porter and the floor waiter?

THE FIRST MAN

Just as easy. The hall porter gets whatever the chambermaid gets, plus twenty-five per cent.—but no more than two marks in any one week. The floor waiter gets thirty pfennigs a day straight, but if you stay only one day he gets half a mark, and if you stay more than a week he gets two marks flat a week after the first week. In some hotels the hall porter don't shine shoes. If he don't he gets just as much as if he does, but then the actual "boots" has to be taken care of. He gets half a mark every two days. Every time you put out an extra pair of shoes he gets fifty per cent. more for that day. If you shine your own shoes, or go without shining them, the "boots" gets half his regular tip, but never less than a mark a week.

THE SECOND MAN

Certainly it seems simple enough. I never knew there was any such system.

THE FIRST MAN

I guess you didn't. Very few do. But it's just because Americans don't know it that these foreign blackmailers shake 'em down. Once you let the port*eer* see that you know the ropes, he'll pass the word on to the others, and you'll be treated like a native.

THE SECOND MAN

I see. But how about the elevator boy? I gave the elevator boy in Dresden two marks and he almost fell on my neck, so I figured that I played the sucker.

THE FIRST MAN

So you did. The rule for elevator boys is still somewhat in the air,

65

because so few of these bum hotels over here have elevators, but you can sort of reason the thing out if you put your mind on it. When you get on a street car in Germany, what tip do you give the conductor?

THE SECOND MAN

Five pfennigs.

THE FIRST MAN

Naturally. That's the tip fixed by custom. You may almost say it's the unwritten law. If you gave the conductor more, he would hand you change. Well, how I reason it out is this way: If five pfennigs is enough for a car conductor, who may carry you three miles, why shouldn't it be enough for the elevator boy, who may carry you only three stories?

THE SECOND MAN

It seems fair, certainly.

THE FIRST MAN

And it *is* fair. So all you have to do is to keep account of the number of times you go up and down in the elevator, and then give the elevator boy five pfennigs for each trip. Say you come down in the morning, go up in the evening, and average one other round trip a day. That makes twenty-eight trips a week. Five times twenty-eight is one mark forty—and there you are.

THE SECOND MAN

I see. By the way, what hotel are you stopping at?

66

THE FIRST MAN

The Goldene Esel.

THE SECOND MAN

How is it?

THE FIRST MAN

Oh, so-so. Ask for oatmeal at breakfast and they send to the livery stable for a peck of oats and ask you please to be so kind as to show them how to make it.

THE SECOND MAN

My hotel is even worse. Last night I got into such a sweat under the big German feather bed that I had to throw it off. But when I asked for a single blanket they didn't have any, so I had to wrap up in bath towels.

THE FIRST MAN

Yes, and you used up every one in town. This morning, when I took a bath, the only towel the chambermaid could find wasn't bigger than a wedding invitation. But while she was hunting around I dried off, so no harm was done.

THE SECOND MAN

Well, that's what a man gets for running around in such one-horse countries. In Leipzig they sat a nigger down beside me at the table. In Amsterdam they had cheese for breakfast. In Munich the head waiter had never heard of buckwheat cakes. In Mannheim they charged me ten pfennigs extra for a cake of soap.

67

THE FIRST MAN

What do you think of the railroad trains over here?

THE SECOND MAN

Rotten. That compartment system is all wrong. If nobody comes into your compartment it's lonesome, and if anybody *does* come in it's too damn sociable. And if you try to stretch out and get some sleep, some ruffian begins singing in the next compartment, or the conductor keeps butting in and jabbering at you.

THE FIRST MAN

But you can say *one* thing for the German trains: they get in on time.

THE SECOND MAN

So they do, but no wonder! They run so slow they can't *help* it. The way I figure it, a German engineer must have a devil of a time holding his engine in. The fact is, he usually can't, and so he has to wait outside every big town until the schedule catches up to him. They say they never have accidents, but is it any more than you expect? Did you ever hear of a mud turtle having an accident?

THE FIRST MAN

Scarcely. As you say, these countries are far behind the times. I saw a fire in Cologne; you would have laughed your head off! It was in a feed store near my hotel, and I got there before the firemen. When they came at last, in their tinpot hats, they got out half a dozen big squirts and rushed into the building with them. Then, when it was out, they put the squirts back into their little express wagon and drove off. Not a line of hose run out, not an engine puffing, not a gong heard, not a soul letting out a whoop! It was more like a

68

Sunday-school picnic than a fire. I guess if these Dutch ever *did* have a civilised blaze, it would scare them to death. But they never have any.

THE SECOND MAN

Well, what can you expect? A country where all the charwomen are men and all the garbage men are women! —

For the moment the two have talked each other out, and so they lounge upon the rail in silence and gaze out over the valley. Anon the gumchewer spits. By now the sun has reached the skyline to the westward and the tops of the ice mountains are in gorgeous conflagration. Scarlets war with golden oranges, and vermilions fade into palpitating pinks. Below, in the valley, the colours begin to fade slowly to a uniform seashell grey. It is a scene of indescribable loveliness; the wild reds of hades splashed riotously upon the cold whites and pale blues of heaven. The night train for Venice, a long line of black coaches, is entering the town. Somewhere below, apparently in the barracks, a sunset gun is fired. After a silence of perhaps two or three minutes, the Americans gather fresh inspiration and resume their conversation.

THE FIRST MAN

I have seen worse scenery.

THE SECOND MAN

Very pretty.

THE FIRST MAN

Yes, sir; it's well worth the money.

THE SECOND MAN

But the Rockies beat it all hollow.

THE FIRST MAN

Oh, of course. They have nothing over here that we can't beat to a whisper. Just consider the Rhine, for instance. The Hudson makes it look like a country creek.

THE SECOND MAN

Yes, you're right. Take away the castles, and not even a German would give a hoot for it. It's not so much what a thing *is* over here as what *reputation* it's got. The whole thing is a matter of press-agenting.

THE FIRST MAN

I agree with you. There's the "beautiful, blue Danube." To me it looks like a sewer. If *it's* blue, then *I'm* green. A man would hesitate to drown himself in such a mud puddle.

THE SECOND MAN

But you hear the bands playing that waltz all your life, and so you spend your good money to come over here to see the river. And when you get back home you don't want to admit that you've been a sucker, so you start touting it from hell to breakfast. And then some other fellow comes over and does the same, and so on and so on.

THE FIRST MAN

Yes, it's all a matter of boosting. Day in and day out you hear about Westminster Abbey. Every English book mentions it; it's in the newspapers almost as much as Jane Addams or Caruso. Well, one day you pack your grip, put on your hat and come over to have a look—and what do you find? A one-horse church full of statues!

And every statue crying for sapolio! You expect to see something magnificent and enormous, something to knock your eye out and send you down for the count. What you do see is a second-rate graveyard under roof. And when you examine into it, you find that two-thirds of the graves haven't even got dead men in them! Whenever a prominent Englishman dies, they put up a statue to him in Westminster Abbey—*no matter where he happens to be buried*! I call that clever advertising. That's the way to get the crowd.

THE SECOND MAN

Yes, these foreigners know the game. They have made millions out of it in Paris. Every time you go to see a musical comedy at home, the second act is laid in Paris, and you see a whole stageful of girls wriggling around, and a lot of old sports having the time of their lives. All your life you hear that Paris is something rich and racy, something that makes New York look like Roanoke, Virginia. Well, you fall for the ballyho and come over to have your fling—and then you find that Paris is largely bunk. I spent a whole week in Paris, trying to find something really awful. I hired one of those Jew guides at five dollars a day and told him to go the limit. I said to him: "Don't mind *me*. I am twenty-one years old. Let me have the genuine goods." But the worst he could show me wasn't half as bad as what I have seen in Chicago. Every night I would say to that Jew: "Come on, now Mr. Cohen; let's get away from these tinhorn shows. Lead me to the real stuff." Well, I believe the fellow did his darndest, but he always fell down. I almost felt sorry for him. In the end, when I paid him off, I said to him: "Save up your money, my boy, and come over to the States. Let me know when you land. I'll show you the sights for nothing. This Baracca Class atmosphere is killing you."

71

THE FIRST MAN

And yet Paris is famous all over the world. No American ever came to Europe without dropping off there to have a look. I once saw the Bal Tabarin crowded with Sunday-school superintendents returning from Jerusalem. And when the sucker gets home he goes around winking and hinting, and so the fake grows. I often think the government ought to take a hand. If the beer is inspected and guaranteed in Germany, why shouldn't the shows be inspected and guaranteed in Paris?

THE SECOND MAN

I guess the trouble is that the Frenchmen themselves never go to their own shows. They don't know what is going on. They see thousands of Americans starting out every night from the Place de l'Opéra and coming back in the morning all boozed up, and so they assume that everything is up to the mark. You'll find the same thing in Washington. No Washingtonian has ever been up to the top of the Washington monument. Once the elevator in the monument was out of commission for two weeks, and yet Washington knew nothing about it. When the news got into the papers at last, it came from Macon, Georgia. Some honeymooner from down there had written home about it, roasting the government.

THE FIRST MAN

Well, me for the good old U. S. A.! These Alps are all right, I guess—but I can't say I like the coffee.

THE SECOND MAN

And it takes too long to get a letter from Jersey City.

THE FIRST MAN

Yes, that reminds me. Just before I started up here this afternoon my wife got the *Ladies' Home Journal* of the month before last. It had been following us around for six weeks, from London to Paris, to Berlin, to Munich, to Vienna, to a dozen other places. Now she's fixed for the night. She won't let up until she's read every word — the advertisements first. And she'll spend all day to-morrow sending off for things; new collar hooks, breakfast foods, complexion soaps and all that sort of junk. Are you married yourself?

THE SECOND MAN

No; not yet.

THE FIRST MAN

Well, then, you don't know how it is. But I guess you play poker.

THE SECOND MAN

Oh, to be sure.

THE FIRST MAN

Well, let's go down into the town and hunt up some quiet barroom and have a civilised evening. This scenery gives me the creeps.

THE SECOND MAN

I'm with you. But where are we going to get any chips?

THE FIRST MAN

Don't worry. I carry a set with me. I made my wife put it in the bottom of my trunk, along with a bottle of real whiskey and a couple of porous plasters. A man can't be too careful when he's away from home— —

They start along the terrace toward the station of the funicular railway. The sun has now disappeared behind the great barrier of ice and the colours of the scene are fast softening. All the scarlets and vermilions are gone; a luminous pink bathes the whole picture in its fairy light. The night train for Venice, leaving the town, appears as a long string of blinking lights. A chill breeze comes from the Alpine vastness to westward. The deep silence of an Alpine night settles down. The two Americans continue their talk until they are out of hearing. The breeze interrupts and obfuscates their words, but now and then half a sentence comes clearly.

THE SECOND MAN

Have you seen any American papers lately?

THE FIRST MAN

Nothing But the Paris *Herald*—if you call *that* a paper.

THE SECOND MAN

How are the Giants making out?

THE FIRST MAN

... bad as usual ... rotten ... shake up ...

THE SECOND MAN

... John McGraw ...

THE FIRST MAN

... homesick ... give five dollars for ...

74

THE SECOND MAN

... whole continent without a single ...

THE FIRST MAN

... glad to get back ... damn tired ...

THE SECOND MAN

... damn ...!

THE FIRST MAN

... *damn* ...!

VII

From the Memoirs of the DevilV

January 6.

And yet, and yet—is not all this contumely a part of my punishment? To be reviled by the righteous as the author of all evil; worse still, to be venerated by the wicked as the accomplice, nay, the instigator, of their sins! A harsh, hard fate! But should I not rejoice that I have been vouchsafed the strength to bear it, that the ultimate mercy is mine? Should I not be full of calm, deep delight that I am blessed with the resignation of the Psalmist (II Samuel XV, 26), the sublime grace of the pious Hezekiah (II Kings XX, 19)? If Hezekiah could bear the cruel visitation of his erring upon his sons, why should I, poor worm that I am, repine?

January 8.

All afternoon I watched the damned filing in. With what horror that spectacle must fill every right-thinking man! Sometimes I think that the worst of all penalties of sin is this: that the sinful actually seem to be glad of their sins (Psalms X, 4). I looked long and earnestly into that endless procession of faces. In not one of them did I see any sign of sorrow or repentance. They marched in defiantly, almost proudly. Ever and anon I heard a snicker, sometimes a downright laugh: there was a coarse buffoonery in the ranks. I turned aside at last, unable to bear it longer. Here they will learn what their laughter is worth! (Eccl. II, 2.)

76

Among them I marked a female, young and fair. How true the words of Solomon: "Favour is deceitful, and beauty is vain!" (Proverbs XXXI, 30.) I could not bring myself to put down upon these pages the whole record of that wicked creature's shameless life. Truly it has been said that "the lips of a strange woman drop as a honeycomb, and her mouth is smoother than oil." (Proverbs V, 3.) One hears of such careers of evil-doing and can scarcely credit them. Can it be that the children of men are so deaf to all the warnings given them, so blind to the vast certainty of their punishment, so ardent in seeking temptation, so lacking in holy fire to resist it? Such thoughts fill me with the utmost distress. Is not the command to a moral life plain enough? Are we not told to "live soberly, righteously, and godly?" (Titus II, 11.) Are we not solemnly warned to avoid the invitation of evil? (Proverbs I, 10.)

January 9.

I have had that strange woman before me and heard her miserable story. It is as I thought. The child of a poor but pious mother, (a widow with six children), she had every advantage of a virtuous, consecrated home. The mother, earning $6 a week, gave 25 cents of it to foreign missions. The daughter, at the tender age of 4, was already a regular attendant at Sabbath-school. The good people of the church took a Christian interest in the family, and one of them, a gentleman of considerable wealth, and an earnest, diligent worker for righteousness, made it his special care to befriend the girl. He took her into his office, treating her almost as one of his own daughters. She served him in the capacity of stenographer, receiving therefor the wage of $7.00 a week, a godsend to that lowly household. How truly, indeed, it has been said: "Verily, there is a reward for the righteous." (Psalms LVIII, 11.)

And now behold how powerful are the snares of evil. (Genesis VI,

12.) There was that devout and saintly man, ripe in good works, a deacon and pillar in the church, a steadfast friend to the needy and erring, a stalwart supporter of his pastor in all forward-looking enterprises, a tower of strength for righteousness in his community, the father of four daughters. And there was that shameless creature, that evil woman, that sinister temptress. With the noisome details I do not concern myself. Suffice it to say that the vile arts of the hussy prevailed over that noble and upright man—that she enticed him, by adroit appeals to his sympathy, into taking her upon automobile rides, into dining with her clandestinely in the private rooms of dubious hotels, and finally into accompanying her upon a despicable, adulterous visit to Atlantic City. And then, seeking to throw upon him the blame for what she chose to call her "wrong," she held him up to public disgrace and worked her own inexorable damnation by taking her miserable life. Well hath the Preacher warned us against the woman whose "heart is snares and nets, and her hands as bands." (Eccl. VII, 26.) Well do we know the wreck and ruin that such agents of destruction can work upon the innocent and trusting. (Revelations XXI, 8; I Corinthians VI, 18; Job XXXI, 12; Hosea IV, 11: Proverbs VI, 26.)

January 11.

We have resumed our evening services—an hour of quiet communion in the failing light. The attendance, alas, is not as gratifying as it might be, but the brethren who gather are filled with holy zeal. It is inspiring to hear their eloquent confessions of guilt and wrongdoing, their trembling protestations of contrition. Several of them are of long experience and considerable proficiency in public speaking. One was formerly a major in the Salvation Army. Another spent twenty years in the Dunkard ministry, finally retiring to devote himself to lecturing on the New Thought. A third was a Y. M. C. A. secretary in Iowa. A fourth was THE FIRST MAN to lift his voice for sex hygiene west of the Mississippi river.

All these men eventually succumbed to temptation, and hence they are here, but I think that no one who has ever glimpsed their secret and inmost souls (as I have during our hours of humble heart-searching together) will fail to testify to their inherent purity of character. After all, it is not what we do but what we have in our hearts that reveals our true worth. (Joshua XXIV, 14.) As David so beautifully puts it, it is "the imagination of the thoughts." (I Chronicles XXIII, 9.) I love and trust these brethren. They are true and earnest Christians. They loathe the temptation to which they succumbed, and deplore the weakness that made them yield. How the memory at once turns to that lovely passage in the Book of Job: "Wherefore I abhor myself, and repent in dust and ashes." Where is there a more exquisite thought in all Holy Writ?

January 14.

I have had that scarlet woman before me, and invited her to join us in our inspiring evening gatherings. For reply she mocked me. Thus Paul was mocked by the Athenians. Thus the children of Bethel mocked Elisha the Prophet (II Kings II, 23). Thus the sinful show their contempt, not only for righteousness itself, but also for its humblest agents and advocates. Nevertheless, I held my temper before her. I indulged in no vain and worldly recriminations. When she launched into her profane and disgraceful tirade against that good and faithful brother, her benefACTOR and victim, I held my peace. When she accused him of foully destroying her, I returned her no harsh words. Instead, I merely read aloud to her those inspiring words from Revelation XIV, 10: "And the evil-doer shall be tormented with fire and brimstone in the presence of the holy

79

angels." And then I smiled upon her and bade her begone. Who am I, that I should hold myself above the most miserable of sinners?

January 18.

Again that immoral woman. I had sent her a few Presbyterian tracts: "The Way to Redemption," "The Story of a Missionary in Polynesia," "The White Slave,"—inspiring and consecrated writings, all of them—comforting to me in many a bitter hour. When she came in I thought it was to ask me to pray with her. (II Chronicles VII, 14.) But her heart, it appears, is still shut to the words of salvation. She renewed her unseemly denunciation of her benefACTOR, and sought to overcome me with her weeping. I found myself strangely drawn toward her—almost pitying her. She approached me, her eyes suffused with tears, her red lips parted, her hair flowing about her shoulders. I felt myself drawn to her. I knew and understood the temptation of that great and good man. But by a powerful effort of the will—or, should I say, by a sudden access of grace?—I recovered and pushed her from me. And then, closing my eyes to shut out the image of her, I pronounced those solemn and awful words: "Vengeance is mine, saith the Lord!" The effect was immediate: she emitted a moan and departed. I had resisted her abhorrent blandishments. (Proverbs I, 10.)

January 25.

I love the Book of Job. Where else in the Scriptures is there a more striking picture of the fate that overtakes those who yield to sin? "They meet with darkness in the day-time, and grope in the noon-day as in the night" (Job V, 14). And further on: "They grope in the dark without light, and he maketh them to stagger like a drunken man" (Job XII, 25). I read these beautiful passages over and over again. They comfort me.

80

That shameless person once more. She sends back the tracts I gave her—torn in halves.

February 3.

That American brother, the former Dunkard, thrilled us with his eloquence at to-night's meeting. In all my days I have heard no more affecting plea for right living. In words that almost seemed to be of fire he set forth the duty of all of us to combat sin wherever we find it, and to scourge the sinner until he foregoes his folly.

"It is not sufficient," he said, "that we keep our own hearts pure: we must also purge the heart of our brother. And if he resist us, let no false sympathy for him stay our hands. We are charged with the care and oversight of his soul. He is in our keeping. Let us seek at first to save him with gentleness, but if he draws back, let us unsheath the sword! We must be deaf to his protests. We must not be deceived by his casuistries. If he clings to his sinning, he must perish."

Cries of "Amen!" arose spontaneously from the little band of consecrated workers. I have never heard a more triumphant call to that Service which is the very heart's blood of righteousness. Who could listen to it, and then stay his hand?

I looked for that scarlet creature. She was not there.

February 7.

I have seen her again. She came, I thought, in all humility. I received her gently, quoting aloud the beautiful words of Paul in Colossians III, 12: "Put on therefore, holy and beloved, bowels of mercies, kindness, humbleness of mind, meekness, long-suffering."

81

And then I addressed her in calm, encouraging tones: "Are you ready, woman, to put away your evil-doing, and forswear your carnalities forevermore? Have you repented of your black and terrible sin? Do you ask for mercy? Have you come in sackcloth and ashes?"

The effect, alas, was not what I planned. Instead of yielding to my entreaty and casting herself down for forgiveness, she yielded to her pride and mocked me! And then, her heart still full of the evils of the flesh, *she tried to tempt me*! She approached me. She lifted up her face to mine. She smiled at me with abominable suggestiveness. She touched me with her garment. She laid her hand upon my arm.... I felt my resolution going from me. I was as one stricken with the palsy. My tongue clave to the roof of my mouth. My hands trembled. I tried to push her from me and could not....

February 10.

In all humility of spirit I set it down. The words burn the paper; the fact haunts me like an evil dream. I yielded to that soulless and abominable creature. I *kissed her*.... And then she laughed, making a mock of me in my weakness, burning me with the hot iron of her scorn, piercing my heart with the daggers of her reviling. Laughed, and slapped my face! Laughed, and spat in my eye! Laughed, *and called me a hypocrite*!...

They have taken her away. *Let her taste the fire!* Let her sin receive its meet and inexorable punishment! Let righteousness prevail! Let her go with "the fearful and unbelieving, the abominable and murderers, the white-slave traders and sorcerers." Off with her to that lake "which burneth with fire and brimstone!" (Revelation XXI, 8.)....

Go, Jezebel! Go, Athaliah! Go, Painted One! Thy sins have found thee out.

February 11.

I spoke myself at to-night's meeting—simple words, but I think their message was not lost. We must wage forever the good fight. We must rout the army of sin from its fortresses....

VIII

Litanies for the Overlooked

I

For Americanos

From scented hotel soap, and from the Boy Scouts; from home cooking, and from pianos with mandolin attachments; from prohibition, and from Odd Fellows' funerals; from Key West cigars, and from cold dinner plates; from transcendentalism, and from the New Freedom; from fat women in straight-front corsets, and from Philadelphia cream cheese; from *The Star-Spangled Banner*, and from the International Sunday-school Lessons; from rubber heels, and from the college spirit; from sulphate of quinine, and from Boston baked beans; from chivalry, and from laparotomy; from the dithyrambs of Herbert Kaufman, and from sport in all its hideous forms; from women with pointed fingernails, and from men with messianic delusions; from the retailers of smutty anecdotes about the Jews, and from the Lake Mohonk Conference; from Congressmen, vice crusaders, and the heresies of Henry Van Dyke; from jokes in the *Ladies' Home Journal*, and from the Revised Statutes of the United States; from Colonial Dames, and from men who boast that they take cold shower-baths every morning; from the Drama League, and from malicious animal magnetism; from ham and eggs, and from the *Weltanschauung* of Kansas; from the theory that a dark cigar is always a strong one, and from the theory that a horse-hair put into a bottle of water will turn into a snake;

from campaigns against profanity, and from the Pentateuch; from anti-vivisection, and from women who do not smoke; from wine-openers, and from Methodists; from Armageddon, and from the belief that a bloodhound never makes a mistake; from sarcerdotal moving-pictures, and from virtuous chorus girls; from bungalows, and from cornets in B flat; from canned soups, and from women who leave everything to one's honor; from detachable cuffs, and from *Lohengrin*; from unwilling motherhood, and from canary birds—good Lord, deliver us!

II

For Hypochondriacs

From adenoids, and from chronic desquamative nephritis; from Shiga's *bacillus*, and from hysterotrachelorrhaphy; from mitral insufficiency, and from Cheyne-Stokes breathing; from the *streptococcus pyogenes*, and from splanchnoptosis; from warts, wens, and the *spirochæte pallida*; from exophthalmic goitre, and from septicopyemia; from poisoning by sewer-gas, and from the *bacillus coli communis*; from anthrax, and from von Recklinghausen's disease; from recurrent paralysis of the laryngeal nerve, and from pityriasis versicolor; from mania-à-potu, and from nephrorrhaphy; from the *leptothrix*, and from colds in the head; from tape-worms, from jiggers and from scurvy; from endocarditis, and from Romberg's masticatory spasm; from hypertrophic stenosis of the pylorus, and from fits; from the *bacillus botulinus*, and from salaam convulsions; from cerebral monoplegia, and from morphinism; from anaphylaxis, and from neuralgia in the eyeball; from dropsy, and from dum-dum fever; from autumnal catarrh, from coryza vasomotoria, from idiosyncratic coryza, from pollen catarrh, from rhinitis sympathetica, from rose cold, from *catarrhus æstivus*, from periodic hyperesthetic rhinitis, from *heuasthma*, from *catarrhe d' été* and from hay-fever—good Lord, deliver us!

III

For Music Lovers

From all piano-players save Paderewski, Godowski and Mark Hambourg; and from the *William Tell* and *1812* overtures; and from bad imitations of Victor Herbert by Victor Herbert; and from persons who express astonishment that Dr. Karl Muck, being a German, is devoid of all bulge, corporation, paunch or leap-tick; and from the saxophone, the piccolo, the cornet and the bagpipes; and from the theory that America has no folk-music; and from all symphonic poems by English composers; and from the tall, willing, horse-chested, ham-handed, quasi-gifted ladies who stagger to their legs in gloomy drawing rooms after bad dinners and poison the air with Tosti's *Good-bye*; and from the low prehensile, godless laryngologists who prostitute their art to the saving of tenors who are happily threatened with loss of voice; and from clarinet cadenzas more than two inches in length; and from the first two acts of *Il Trovatore*; and from such fluffy, xanthous whiskers as Lohengrins wear; and from sentimental old maids who sink into senility lamenting that Brahms never wrote an opera; and from programme music, with or without notes; and from Swiss bell-ringers, Vincent D'Indy, the Paris Opera, and Elgar's *Salut d'Amour*; and from the doctrine that Massenet was a greater composer than Dvořák; and from Italian bands and *Schnellpostdoppelschraubendampfer* orchestras; and from Raff's *Cavatina* and all of Tschaikowsky except ten per centum; and from prima donna conductors who change their programmes without notice, and so get all the musical critics into a sweat; and from the abandoned hussies who sue tenors for breach of promise; and from all alleged musicians who do not shrivel to the size of five-cent cigars whenever they think of old Josef Haydn—good Lord, deliver us!

IV

For Hangmen

From clients who delay the exercises by pausing to make long and irrelevant speeches from the scaffold, or to sing depressing Methodist hymns; and from medical examiners who forget their stethoscopes, and clamor for waits while messenger boys are sent for them; and from official witnesses who faint at the last minute, and have to be hauled out by the deputy sheriffs; and from undertakers who keep looking at their watches and hinting obscenely that they have other engagements at 10:30; and from spiritual advisers who crowd up at the last minute and fall through the trap with the condemned—good Lord, deliver us!

V

For Magazine Editors

From Old Subscribers who write in to say that the current number is the worst magazine printed since the days of the New York *Galaxy*; and from elderly poetesses who have read all the popular text-books of sex hygiene, and believe all the bosh in them about the white slave trade, and so suspect the editor, and even the publisher, of sinister designs; and from stories in which a rising young district attorney gets the dead wood upon a burly political boss named Terrence O'Flaherty, and then falls in love with Mignon, his daughter, and has to let him go; and from stories in which a married lady, just about to sail for Capri with her husband's old *Corpsbruder*, is dissuaded from her purpose by the news that her husband has lost $700,000 in Wall Street and is on his way home to weep on her shoulder; and from one-act plays in which young Cornelius Van Suydam comes home from The Club at 11:55 P. M. on Christmas Eve, dismisses Dodson, his Man, with the compliments of the season, and draws up his chair before the open fire to dream of his girl, thus preparing the way for the entrance of Maxwell, the starving burglar, and for the scene in which Maxwell's little daughter, Fifi, following him up the fire-escape, pleads with him to give up his evil courses; and from poems about war in which it is argued that thousands of young men are always killed, and that their mothers regret to hear of it; and from essays of a sweet and whimsical character, in which the author refers to himself as "we," and ends by quoting Bergson, Washington Irving or Agnes Repplier; and from epigrams based on puns, good or bad; and from stories beginning, "It was the autumn of the year 1950"; and from stories embodying quotations from Omar Khayyam, and full of a mellow pessimism; and from stories in which the gay nocturnal life of the Latin Quarter is described by an author living in Dubuque, Iowa; and from stories of thought transference, mental healing and haunted houses; and from newspaper stories in which a cub reporter solves the mystery of the Snodgrass murder and is promoted to dramatic critic on the field, or in which a city editor who smokes a corn-cob pipe falls in love with a sob-sister; and from stories about trained nurses, young dramatists, baseball players, heroic locomotive engineers, settlement workers, clergymen, yeggmen, cowboys, Italians, employés of the Hudson Bay Company and great detectives; and from stories in which the dissolute son of a department store owner tries to seduce a working girl in his father's employ and then goes on the water wagon and marries her as a tribute to her virtue; and from stories in which the members of a yachting party are wrecked on a desert island in the

South Pacific, and the niece of the owner of the yacht falls in love with the bo'sun; and from manuscripts accompanied by documents certifying that the incidents and people described are real, though cleverly disguised; and from authors who send in saucy notes when their offerings are returned with insincere thanks; and from lady authors who appear with satirical letters of introduction from the low, raffish rogues who edit rival magazines—good Lord, deliver us!

IX

Asepsis. A Deduction in Scherzo Form

Characters:

A Clergyman
A Bride
Four Bridesmaids
A Bridegroom
A Best Man
The Usual Crowd

Place — *The surgical amphitheatre in a hospital.*
Time — *Noon of a fair day.*

Seats rising in curved tiers. The operating pit paved with white tiles. The usual operating table has been pushed to one side, and in place of it there is a small glass-topped bedside table. On it, a large roll of aseptic cotton, several pads of gauze, a basin of bichloride, a pair of clinical thermometers in a little glass of alcohol, a dish of green soap, a beaker of two per cent. carbolic acid, and a microscope. In one corner stands a sterilizer, steaming pleasantly like a tea kettle. There are no decorations — no flowers, no white ribbons, no satin cushions. To the left a door leads into the Anesthetic Room. A pungent smell of ether, nitrous oxide, iodine, chlorine, wet laundry and scorched gauze. Temperature: 98.6 degrees Fahr.

THE CLERGYMAN *is discovered standing behind the table in an expectant attitude. He is in the long white coat of a surgeon, with his head wrapped in white gauze and a gauze respirator over his mouth. His chunkiness suggests a fat, middle-aged Episcopal rector, but it is impossible to see either his face or his vestments. He wears rubber gloves of a dirty orange color, evidently much used.* THE BRIDEGROOM *and* The Best Man *have just emerged from the Anesthetic Room and are standing before him. Both are dressed exactly as he is, save that* THE BRIDEGROOM's *rubber gloves are white. The benches running up the amphitheatre are filled with spectators, chiefly women. They are in dingy oilskins, and most of them also wear respirators.*

After a long and uneasy pause The Bride *comes in from the Anesthetic Room on the arm of her* Father, *with* the Four Bridesmaids *following by twos. She is dressed in what appears to be white linen, with a long veil of aseptic gauze. The gauze testifies to its late and careful sterilization by yellowish scorches. There is a white rubber glove upon* the Bride's *right hand, but that belonging to her left hand has been removed. Her* Father *is dressed like* the Best Man. *The Four Bridesmaids are in the garb of surgical nurses, with their hair completely concealed by turbans of gauze. As* the Bride *takes her place before* THE CLERGYMAN, *with* THE BRIDEGROOM *at her right, there is a faint, snuffling murmur among the spectators. It hushes suddenly as* THE CLERGYMAN *clears his throat.*

THE CLERGYMAN

(In sonorous, booming tones, somewhat muffled by his respirator.) Dearly beloved, we are gathered here together in the face of this company to join together this man and this woman in holy matrimony, which is commended by God to be honorable among men, and therefore is not to be entered into inadvisedly or carelessly, or without due surgical precautions, but reverently, cleanly, sterilely, soberly, scientifically, and with the nearest practicable approach to

91

bacteriological purity. Into this laudable and non-infectious state these two persons present come now to be joined and quarantined. If any man can show just cause, either clinically or microscopically, why they may not be safely sutured together, let him now come forward with his charts, slides and cultures, or else hereafter forever hold his peace.

(*Several spectators shuffle their feet, and an old maid giggles, but no one comes forward.*)

THE CLERGYMAN

(*To* the Bride *and* Bridegroom): I require and charge both of you, as ye will answer in the dreadful hour of autopsy, when the secrets of all lives shall be disclosed, that if either of you know of any lesion, infection, malaise, congenital defect, hereditary taint or other impediment, why ye may not be lawfully joined together in eugenic matrimony, ye do now confess it. For be ye well assured that if any persons are joined together otherwise than in a state of absolute chemical and bacteriological innocence, their marriage will be septic, unhygienic, pathogenic and toxic, and eugenically null and void.

(THE BRIDEGROOM *hands over a long envelope, from which* THE CLERGYMAN *extracts a paper bearing a large red seal.*)

THE CLERGYMAN

(*Reading*): We, and each of us, having subjected the bearer, John Doe, to a rigid clinical and laboratory examination, in accordance with Form B-3 of the United States Public Health Service, do hereby certify that, to the best of our knowledge and belief, he is free from all disease, taint, defect, deformity or hereditary blemish, saving as noted herein. Temperature *per ora*, 98.6. Pulse, 76, strong.

Respiration, 28.5. Wassermann,—2. Hb., 114%. Phthalein, 1st. hr., 46%; 2nd hr., 21%. W. B. C., 8,925. Free gastric HCl, 11.5%. No stasis. No lactic acid. Blood pressure, 122/77. No albuminuria. No glycosuria. Lumbar puncture: clear fluid, normal pressure.

Defects Noted. 1. Left heel jerk feeble. 2. Caries in five molars. 3. Slight acne rosacea. 4. Slight inequality of curvature in meridians of right cornea. 5. Nicotine stain on right forefinger, extending to middle of second phalanx.

(*Signed*)

Sigismund Kraus, M.D.

Wm. T. Robertson, M.D.

James Simpson, M.D.

Subscribed and sworn to before me, a Notary Public for the Borough of Manhattan, City of New York, State of New York.

(*Seal*) Abraham Lechetitsky.

So much for the reading of the minutes. (*To* the Bride): Now for yours, my dear.

(The Bride *hands up a similar envelope, from which* THE CLERGYMAN *extracts a similar document. But instead of reading it aloud, he delicately runs his eye through it in silence.*)

THE CLERGYMAN

(*The reading finished*) Very good. Very creditable. You must see some good oculist about your astigmatism, my dear. Surely you want to avoid glasses. Come to my study on your return and I'll give you the name of a trustworthy man. And now let us proceed with the ceremony of marriage. (*To* THE BRIDEGROOM): John, wilt thou have this woman to be thy wedded wife, to live together in the holy state of eugenic matrimony? Wilt thou love her, comfort her, protect her from all protozoa and bacteria, and keep her in good health; and, forsaking all other, keep thee unto her only, so long as ye both shall live? If so, hold out your tongue.

(THE BRIDEGROOM *holds out his tongue and* THE CLERGYMAN *inspects it critically.*)

THE CLERGYMAN

(*Somewhat dubiously*) Fair. I have seen worse.... Do you smoke?

THE BRIDEGROOM

(*Obviously lying*) Not much.

THE CLERGYMAN

Well, *how* much?

THE BRIDEGROOM

Say ten cigarettes a day.

THE CLERGYMAN

And the stain noted on your right posterior phalanx by the learned medical examiners?

THE BRIDEGROOM

Well, say fifteen.

THE CLERGYMAN

(*Waggishly*) Or twenty to be safe. Better taper off to ten. At all events, make twenty the limit. How about the booze?

94

THE BRIDEGROOM

(*Virtuously*) Never!

THE CLERGYMAN

What! Never?

THE BRIDEGROOM

Well, never again!

THE CLERGYMAN

So they *all* say. The answer is almost part of the liturgy. But have a care, my dear fellow! The true eugenist eschews the wine cup. In every hundred children of a man who ingests one fluid ounce of alcohol a day, six will be left-handed, twelve will be epileptics and nineteen will suffer from adolescent albuminuria, with delusions of persecution.... Have you ever had anthrax?

THE BRIDEGROOM

Not yet.

THE CLERGYMAN

Eczema?

THE BRIDEGROOM

No.

THE CLERGYMAN

Pott's disease?

THE BRIDEGROOM

No.

THE CLERGYMAN

Cholelithiasis?

THE BRIDEGROOM

No.

THE CLERGYMAN

Do you have a feeling of distention after meals?

THE BRIDEGROOM

No.

THE CLERGYMAN

Have you a dry, hacking cough?

THE BRIDEGROOM

Not at present.

THE CLERGYMAN

Are you troubled with insomnia?

THE BRIDEGROOM

No.

THE CLERGYMAN

Dyspepsia?

THE BRIDEGROOM

No.

THE CLERGYMAN

Agoraphobia?

THE BRIDEGROOM

No.

THE CLERGYMAN

Do you bolt your food?

THE BRIDEGROOM

No.

THE CLERGYMAN

Have you lightning pains in the legs?

THE BRIDEGROOM

No.

THE CLERGYMAN

Are you a bleeder? Have you hæmophilia?

THE BRIDEGROOM

No.

THE CLERGYMAN

Erthrocythæmia? Nephroptosis? Fibrinous bronchitis? Salpingitis? Pylephlebitis? Answer yes or no.

97

THE BRIDEGROOM

No. No. No. No. No.

THE CLERGYMAN

Have you ever been refused life insurance? If so, when, by what company or companies, and why?

THE BRIDEGROOM

No.

THE CLERGYMAN

What is a staphylococcus?

THE BRIDEGROOM

No.

THE CLERGYMAN

(*Sternly*) What?

THE BRIDEGROOM

(*Nervously*) Yes.

THE CLERGYMAN

(*Coming to the rescue*) Wilt them have this woman et cetera? Answer yes or no.

THE BRIDEGROOM

I will.

THE CLERGYMAN

(*Turning to* The Bride) Mary, wilt thou have this gentleman to be thy wedded husband, to live together in the holy state of aseptic matrimony? Wilt thou love him, serve him, protect him from all adulterated victuals, and keep him hygienically clothed; and forsaking all others, keep thee only unto him, so long as ye both shall live? If so— —

THE BRIDE

(*Instantly and loudly*) I will.

THE CLERGYMAN

Not so fast! First, there is the little ceremony of the clinical thermometers. (*He takes up one of the thermometers.*) Open your mouth, my dear. (*He Inserts the thermometer.*) Now hold it there while you count one hundred and fifty. And you, too. (*To* THE BRIDEGROOM.) I had almost forgotten you. (THE BRIDEGROOM *opens his mouth and the other thermometer is duly planted. While the two are counting,* THE CLERGYMAN *attempts to turn back one of* The Bride's *eyelids, apparently searching for trachoma, but his rubber gloves impede the operation and so he gives it up. It is now time to read the thermometers.* THE BRIDEGROOM's *is first removed.*)

THE CLERGYMAN

(*Reading the scale*) Ninety-nine point nine. Considering everything, not so bad. (*Then he removes and reads* The Bride's.) Ninety-eight point six. Exactly normal. Cool, collected, at ease. The classical self-possession of the party of the second part. And now, my dear, may I ask you to hold out your tongue? (The Bride *does so.*)

THE CLERGYMAN

Perfect.... There; that will do. Put it back.... And now for a few questions—just a few. First, do you use opiates in any form?

THE BRIDE

No.

THE CLERGYMAN

Have you ever had goitre?

THE BRIDE

No.

THE CLERGYMAN

Yellow fever?

THE BRIDE

No.

THE CLERGYMAN

Hæmatomata?

THE BRIDE

No.

THE CLERGYMAN

Siriasis or tachycardia?

THE BRIDE

No.

THE CLERGYMAN

What did your maternal grandfather die of?

THE BRIDE

Of chronic interstitial nephritis.

THE CLERGYMAN

(*Interested*) Ah, our old friend Bright's! A typical case, I take, with the usual polyuria, œdema of the glottis, flame-shaped retinal hemorrhages and cardiac dilatation?

THE BRIDE

Exactly.

THE CLERGYMAN

And terminating, I suppose, with the classical uræmic symptoms—dyspnœa, convulsions, uræmic amaurosis, coma and collapse?

THE BRIDE

Including Cheyne-Stokes breathing.

THE CLERGYMAN

Ah, most interesting! A protean and beautiful malady! But at the moment, of course, we can't discuss it profitably. Perhaps later on.... Your father, I assume, is alive?

THE BRIDE

(*Indicating him*) Yes.

THE CLERGYMAN

Well, then, let us proceed. Who giveth this woman to be married to this man?

THE BRIDE'S FATHER

(*With a touch of stage fright.*) I do.

THE CLERGYMAN

(*Reassuringly*) You are in good health?

THE BRIDE'S FATHER

Yes.

THE CLERGYMAN

No dizziness in the morning?

THE BRIDE'S FATHER

No.

THE CLERGYMAN

No black spots before the eyes?

THE BRIDE'S FATHER

No.

THE CLERGYMAN

No vague pains in the small of the back?

THE BRIDE'S FATHER

No.

THE CLERGYMAN

Gout?

THE BRIDE'S FATHER

No.

THE CLERGYMAN

Chilblains?

THE BRIDE'S FATHER

No.

THE CLERGYMAN

Sciatica?

THE BRIDE'S FATHER

No.

THE CLERGYMAN

Buzzing in the ears?

THE BRIDE'S FATHER

No.

THE CLERGYMAN

Myopia? Angina pectoris?

THE BRIDE'S FATHER

No.

THE CLERGYMAN

Malaria? Marasmus? Chlorosis? Tetanus? Quinsy? Housemaid's knee?

103

THE BRIDE'S FATHER

No.

THE CLERGYMAN

You had measles, I assume, in your infancy?

THE BRIDE'S FATHER

Yes.

THE CLERGYMAN

Chicken pox? Mumps? Scarlatina? Cholera morbus? Diphtheria?

THE BRIDE'S FATHER

Yes. Yes. No. Yes. No.

THE CLERGYMAN

You are, I assume, a multipara?

THE BRIDE'S FATHER

A what?

THE CLERGYMAN

That is to say, you have had more than one child?

THE BRIDE'S FATHER

No.

THE CLERGYMAN

(*Professionally*) How sad! You will miss her!

THE BRIDE'S FATHER

One job like this is en— —

THE CLERGYMAN

(*Interrupting suavely*) But let us proceed. The ceremony must not be lengthened unduly, however interesting. We now approach the benediction.

(*Dipping his gloved hands into the basin of bichloride, he joins the right hands of* The Bride *and* THE BRIDEGROOM.)

THE CLERGYMAN

(*To* THE BRIDEGROOM) Repeat after me: "I, John, take thee, Mary, to be my wedded and aseptic wife, to have and to hold from this day forward, for better, for worse, for richer, for poorer, in sickness, convalescence, relapse and health, to love and to cherish, till death do us part; and thereto I plight thee my troth."

(THE BRIDEGROOM *duly repeats the formula,* THE CLERGYMAN *now looses their hands, and after another dip into the bichloride, joins them together again.*)

THE CLERGYMAN

(*To* The Bride) Repeat after me: "I, Mary, take thee, John, to be my aseptic and eugenic husband, to have and to hold from this day forward, for better, for worse, for richer, for poorer, to love, to cherish and to nurse, till death do us part; and thereto I give thee my troth."

(The Bride *duly promises. The Best Man* then hands over the ring, which THE CLERGYMAN *drops into the bichloride. It turns green. He fishes it up again, wipes it dry with a piece of aseptic cotton and presents it to* THE

BRIDEGROOM, *who places it upon the third finger of* The Bride's *left hand. Then* THE CLERGYMAN *goes on with the ceremony,* THE BRIDEGROOM *repeating after him.*)

THE CLERGYMAN

Repeat after me: "With this sterile ring I thee wed, and with all my worldly goods I thee endow."

(THE CLERGYMAN *then joins the hands of* The Bride *and* Bridegroom *once more, and dipping his own right hand into the bichloride, solemnly sprinkles the pair.*)

THE CLERGYMAN

Those whom God hath joined together, let no pathogenic organism put asunder. (*To the assembled company.*) Forasmuch as John and Mary have consented together in aseptic wedlock, and have witnessed the same by the exchange of certificates, and have given and pledged their troth, and have declared the same by giving and receiving an aseptic ring, I pronounce that they are man and wife. In the name of Mendel, of Galton, of Havelock Ellis and of David Starr Jordan. Amen.

(The Bride *and* Bridegroom *now kiss, for the first and last time, after which they gargle with two per cent carbolic and march out of the room, followed by* THE BRIDE'S FATHER *and the spectators. The Best Man, before departing after them, hands* THE CLERGYMAN *a ten-dollar gold-piece in a small phial of twenty per cent bichloride.* THE CLERGYMAN, *after pocketing it, washes his hands with green soap. The Bridesmaids proceed to clean up the room with the remaining bichloride. This done, they and* THE CLERGYMAN *go out. As soon as they are gone, the operating table is pushed back into place by an orderly, a patient is brought in, and a surgeon proceeds to cut off his leg.*)

X

Tales of the Moral and Pathological

I

The Rewards of Science

Once upon a time there was a surgeon who spent seven years perfecting an extraordinarily delicate and laborious operation for the cure of a rare and deadly disease. In the process he wore out $400 worth of knives and saws and used up $6,000 worth of ether, splints, guinea pigs, homeless dogs and bichloride of mercury. His board and lodging during the seven years came to $2,875. Finally he got a patient and performed the operation. It took eight hours and cost him $17 more than his fee of $20....

One day, two months after the patient was discharged as cured, the surgeon stopped in his rambles to observe a street parade. It was the annual turnout of Good Hope Lodge, No. 72, of the Patriotic Order of American Rosicrucians. The cured patient, marching as Supreme Worthy Archon, wore a lavender baldric, a pea-green sash, an aluminum helmet and scarlet gauntlets, and carried an ormolu sword and the blue polka-dot flag of a rear-admiral....

With a low cry the surgeon jumped down a sewer and was seen no more.

The Incomparable Physician

The eminent physician, Yen Li-Shen, being called in the middle of the night to the bedside of the rich tax-gatherer, Chu Yi-Foy, found his distinguished patient suffering from a spasm of the liver. An examination of the pulse, tongue, toe-nails, and hair-roots revealing the fact that the malady was caused by the presence of a multitude of small worms in the blood, the learned doctor forthwith dispatched his servant to his surgery for a vial of gnats' eyes dissolved in the saliva of men executed by strangling, that being the remedy advised by Li Tan-Kien and other high authorities for the relief of this painful and dangerous condition.

When the servant returned the patient was so far gone that Cheyne-Stokes breathing had already set in, and so the doctor decided to administer the whole contents of the vial—an heroic dose, truly, for it has been immemorially held that even so little as the amount that will cling to the end of a horse hair is sufficient to cure. Alas, in his professional zeal and excitement, the celebrated pathologist permitted his hand to shake like a myrtle leaf in a Spring gale, and so he dropped not only the contents of the vial, but also the vial itself down the œsophagus of his moribund patient.

The accident, however, did not impede the powerful effects of this famous remedy. In ten minutes Chu Yi-Foy was so far recovered that he asked for a plate of rice stewed with plums, and by morning he was able to leave his bed and receive the reports of his spies, informers and extortioners. That day he sent for Dr. Yen and in token of his gratitude, for he was a just and righteous man, settled upon him in due form of law, and upon his heirs and assigns in perpetuity, the whole rents, rates, imposts and taxes, amounting to no less than ten thousand Hangkow taels a year, of two of the streets occupied by money-changers, bird-cage makers and public women in the town of Szu-Loon, and of the related alleys, courts and lanes. And Dr. Yen, with his old age and the old age of his seven sons and thirty-one grandsons now safely provided for, retired from the practise of his art, and devoted himself to a tedious scientific inquiry (long the object of his passionate aspiration) into the precise physiological relation between gravel in the lower lobe of the heart and the bursting of arteries in the arms and legs.

So passed many years, while Dr. Yen pursued his researches and sent his annual reports of progress to the Academy of Medicine at Chan-Si, and Chu Yi-Foy increased his riches and his influence, so that his arm reached out from the mountains to the sea. One day, in his eightieth year, Chu Yi-Foy fell ill again, and, having no confidence in any other physician, sent once more for the learned and now venerable Dr. Yen.

"I have a pain," he said, "in my left hip, where the stomach dips down over the spleen. A large knob has formed there. A lizard, perhaps, has got into me. Or perhaps a small hedge-hog."

Dr. Yen thereupon made use of the test for lizards and hedge-hogs—to wit, the application of madder dye to the Adam's apple, turning it lemon yellow if any sort of reptile is within, and violet if there is a mammal—but it failed to operate as the books describe. Being thus led to suspect a misplaced and wild-growing bone, perhaps from the vertebral column, the doctor decided to have recourse to surgery, and so, after the proper propitiation of the gods, he administered to his eminent patient a draught of opium water, and having excluded the wailing women of the household from the sick chamber, he cut into the protuberance with a small, sharp knife, and soon had the mysterious object in his hand.... It

was the vial of dissolved gnats' eyes—*still full and tightly corked*!
Worse, it was *not* the vial of dissolved gnats' eyes, but a vial of
common burdock juice—the remedy *for infants griped by their
mothers' milk*....

But when the eminent Chu Yi-Foy, emerging from his benign
stupor, made a sign that he would gaze upon the cause of his
distress, it was a bone that Dr. Yen Li-Shen showed him—an
authentic bone, ovoid and evil-looking—and lately the knee cap of
one Ho Kwang, brass maker in the street of Szchen-Kiang. Dr. Yen
carried this bone in his girdle to keep off the black, blue and yellow
plagues. Chu Yi-Foy, looking upon it, wept the soft, grateful tears of
an old man.

"This is twice," he said, "that you, my learned friend, have saved
my life. I have hitherto given you, in token of my gratitude, the
rents, rates, imposts and taxes, of two streets, and of the related
alleys, courts and lanes. I now give you the weight of that bone in
diamonds, in rubies, in pearls or in emeralds, as you will. And
whichever of the four you choose, I give you the other three also.
For is it not said by K'ung Fu-tsze, 'The good physician bestows
what the gods merely promise'?"

And Dr. Yen Li-Shen lowered his eyes and bowed. But he was too
old in the healing art to blush.

III

Neighbours

Once I lay in hospital a fortnight while an old man died by inches
across the hall. Apparently a very painful, as it was plainly a very
tedious business. I would hear him breathing heavily for fifteen or
twenty minutes, and then he would begin shrieking in agony and

yelling for his orderly: "Charlie! Charlie! Charlie!" Now and then a nurse would come into my room and report progress: "The old fellow's kidneys have given up; he can't last the night," or, "I suppose the next choking spell will fetch him." Thus he fought his titanic fight with the gnawing rats of death, and thus I lay listening, myself quickly recovering from a sanguinary and indecent operation.... Did the shrieks of that old man startle me, worry me, torture me, set my nerves on edge? Not at all. I had my meals to the accompaniment of piteous yells to God, but day by day I ate them more heartily. I lay still in bed and read a book or smoked a cigar. I damned my own twinges and fading malaises. I argued ignorantly with the surgeons. I made polite love to the nurses who happened in. At night I slept soundly, the noise retreating benevolently as I dropped off. And when the old fellow died at last, snarling and begging for mercy with his last breath, the unaccustomed stillness made me feel lonesome and sad, like a child robbed of a tin whistle.... But when a young surgeon came in half an hour later, and, having dined to his content, testified to it by sucking his teeth, cold shudders ran through me from stem to stern.

IV

From the Chart

Temperature: 99.7. Respiration: rising to 65 and then suddenly suspended. The face is flushed, and the eyes are glazed and half-closed. There is obviously a sub-normal reaction to external stimuli. A fly upon the ear is unnoticed. The auditory nerve is anesthetic. There is a swaying of the whole body and an apparent failure of co-ordination, probably the effect of some disturbance in the semi-circular canals of the ear. The hands tremble and then clutch wildly. The head is inclined forward as if to approach some object on a level with the shoulder. The mouth stands partly open, and the lips

111

are puckered and damp. Of a sudden there is a sound as of a deep and labored inspiration, suggesting the upward curve of Cheyne-Stokes breathing. Then comes silence for 40 seconds, followed by a quick relaxation of the whole body and a sharp gasp....

One of the internes has kissed a nurse.

V

The Interior Hierarchy

The world awaits that pundit who will study at length the relative respectability of the inward parts of man—his pipes and bellows, his liver and lights. The inquiry will take him far into the twilight zones of psychology. Why is the vermiform appendix so much more virtuous and dignified than its next-door neighbor, the cæcum? Considered physiologically, anatomically, pathologically, surgically, the cæcum is the decenter of the two. It has more cleanly habits; it is more beautiful; it serves a more useful purpose; it brings its owner less often to the doors of death. And yet what would one think of a lady who mentioned her cæcum? But the appendix—ah, the appendix! The appendix is pure, polite, ladylike, even noble. It confers an unmistakable stateliness, a stamp of position, a social consequence upon its possessor. And, by one of the mysteries of viscerology, it confers even *more* stateliness upon its *ex*-possessor!

Alas, what would you! Why is the stomach such a libertine and outlaw in England, and so highly respectable in the United States? No Englishman of good breeding, save he be far gone in liquor, ever mentions his stomach in the presence of women, clergymen, or the Royal Family. To avoid the necessity—for Englishmen, too, are subject to the colic—he employs various far-fetched euphemisms, among them, the poetical Little Mary. No such squeamishness is known in America. The American discusses his stomach as freely as he discusses his business. More, he regards its name with a degree of respect verging upon reverence—and so he uses it as a euphemism for the whole region from the diaphragm to the pelvic arch. Below his heart he has only a stomach and a vermiform appendix.

In the Englishman that large region is filled entirely by his liver, at least in polite conversation. He never mentions his kidneys save to his medical adviser, but he will tell even a parlor maid that he is feeling liverish. "Sorry, old chap; I'm not up to it. Been seedy for a fortnight. Touch of liver, I dessay. Never felt quite fit since I came Home. Bones full of fever. Damned old liver always kicking up. Awfully sorry, old fellow. Awsk me again. Glad to, pon my word." But never the American! Nay, the American keeps his liver for his secret thoughts. Hobnailed it may be, and the most interesting thing within his frontiers, but he would blush to mention it to a lady.

Myself intensely ignorant of anatomy, and even more so of the punctilio, I yet attempted, one rainy day, a roster of the bodily parts in the order of their respectability. Class I was small and exclusive; when I had put in the heart, the brain, the hair, the eyes and the vermiform appendix, I had exhausted all the candidates. Here were the five aristocrats, of dignity even in their diseases—appendicitis, angina pectoris, aphasia, acute alcoholism, astigmatism: what a row of a's! Here were the dukes, the cardinals, nay, the princes of the blood. Here were the supermembers; the beyond-parts.

In Class II I found a more motley throng, led by the collar-bone on the one hand and the tonsils on the other. And in Class III—but let me present my classification and have done:

113

CLASS II

Collar-bone
Stomach (American)
Liver (English)
Bronchial tubes
Arms (excluding elbows)
Tonsils
Vocal chords
Ears
Cheeks
Chin

CLASS III

Elbows
Ankles
Aorta
Teeth (if natural)
Shoulders
Windpipe
Lungs
Neck
Jugular vein

CLASS IV

Stomach (English)
Liver (American)
Solar plexus

114

Hips
Calves
Pleura
Nose
Feet (bare)
Shins

CLASS V

Teeth (if false)
Heels
Toes
Kidneys
Knees
Diaphragm
Thyroid gland
Legs (female)
Scalp

CLASS VI

Thighs
Paunch
Œsophagus
Spleen
Pancreas
Gall-bladder
Cæcum

I made two more classes, VII and VIII, but they entered into anatomical details impossible of discussion in a book designed to be read aloud at the domestic hearth. Perhaps I shall print them in the *Medical Times* at some future time. As my classes stand, they present mysteries enough. Why should the bronchial tubes (Class II) be so much lordlier than the lungs (Class III) to which they lead? And why should the œsophagus (Class VI) be so much *less* lordly than the stomach (Class II in the United States, Class IV in England) to which *it* leads? And yet the fact in each case is known to us all. To have a touch of bronchitis is almost fashionable; to have pneumonia is merely bad luck. The stomach, at least in America, is so respectable that it dignifies even seasickness, but I have never heard of any decent man who ever had any trouble with his œsophagus.

If you wish a short cut to a strange organ's standing, study its diseases. Generally speaking, they are sure indices. Let us imagine a problem: What is the relative respectability of the hair and the scalp, close neighbors, offspring of the same osseous tissue? Turn to baldness and dandruff, and you have your answer. To be bald is no more than a genial jocosity, a harmless foible—but to have dandruff is almost as bad as to have beri-beri. Hence the fact that the hair is in Class I, while the scalp is at the bottom of Class V. So again and again. To break one's collar-bone (Class II) is to be in harmony with the nobility and gentry; to crack one's shin (Class IV) is merely vulgar. And what a difference between having one's tonsils cut out (Class II) and getting a new set of false teeth (Class V)!

Wherefore? Why? To what end? Why is the stomach so much more respectable (even in England) than the spleen; the liver (even in America) than the pancreas; the windpipe than the œsophagus; the pleura than the diaphragm? Why is the collar-bone the undisputed king of the osseous frame? One can understand the supremacy of

116

the heart: it plainly bosses the whole vascular system. But why do the bronchial tubes wag the lungs? Why is the chin superior to the nose? The ankles to the shins? The solar plexus to the gall-bladder?

I am unequal to the penetration of this great ethical, æsthetical and sociological mystery. But in leaving it, let me point to another and antagonistic one: to wit, that which concerns those viscera of the lower animals that we use for food. The kidneys in man are far down the scale—far down in Class V, along with false teeth, the scalp and the female leg. But the kidneys of the beef steer, the calf, the sheep, or whatever animal it is whose kidneys we eat—the kidneys of this creature are close to the borders of Class I. What is it that young Capt. Lionel Basingstoke, M.P., always orders when he drops in at Gatti's on his way from his chambers in the Albany to that flat in Tyburnia where Mrs. Vaughn-Grimsby is waiting for him to rescue her from her *cochon* of a husband? What else but deviled kidneys? Who ever heard of a gallant young English seducer who did't eat deviled kidneys—not now and then, not only on Sundays and legal holidays, but every day, every evening?

Again, and by way of postscript No. 2, concentrate your mind upon sweetbreads. Sweetbreads are made in Chicago of the pancreases of horned cattle. From Portland to Portland they belong to the first class of refined delicatessen. And yet, on the human plane, the pancreas is in Class VI, along with the cæcum and the paunch. And, contrariwise, there is tripe—"the stomach of the ox or of some other ruminant." The stomach of an American citizen belongs to Class II, and even the stomach of an Englishman is in Class IV, but tripe is far down in Class VIII. And chitterlings—the excised vermiform appendix of the cow. Of all the towns in Christendom, Richmond, Va., is the only one wherein a self-respecting white man would dare to be caught wolfing a chitterling in public.

117

XI

The Jazz Webster

ACTOR. One handicapped more by a wooden leg than by a wooden head.

ADULTERY. Democracy applied to love.

ALIMONY. The ransom that the happy pay to the devil.

ANTI-VIVISECTIONIST. One who gags at a guinea-pig and swallows a baby.

ARCHBISHOP. A Christian ecclesiastic of a rank superior to that attained by Christ.

ARGUMENT. A means of persuasion. The agents of Argumentation under a democracy, in the order of their potency, are (a) whiskey, (b) beer, (c) cigars, (d) tears.

AXIOM. Something that everyone believes. When everyone begins to believe anything it ceases to be true. For example, the notion that the homeliest girl in the party is the safest.

BALLOT BOX. The altar of democracy. The cult served upon it is the worship of jackals by jackasses.

BREVITY. The quality that makes cigarettes, speeches, love affairs and ocean voyages bearable.

CELEBRITY. One who is known to many persons he is glad he doesn't know.

118

CHAUTAUQUA. A place in which persons who are not worth talking to listen to that which is not worth hearing.

CHRISTIAN. One who believes that God notes the fall of a sparrow and is shocked half to death by the fall of a Sunday-school superintendent; one who is willing to serve three Gods, but draws the line at one wife.

CHRISTIAN SCIENCE. The theory that, since the sky rockets following a wallop in the eye are optical delusions, the wallop itself is a delusion and the eye another.

CHURCH. A place in which gentlemen who have never been to Heaven brag about it to persons who will never get there.

CIVILIZATION. A concerted effort to remedy the blunders and check the practical joking of God.

CLERGYMAN. A ticket speculator outside the gates of Heaven.

CONSCIENCE. The inner voice which warns us that someone is looking.

CONFIDENCE. The feeling that makes one believe a man, even when one knows that one would lie in his place.

COURTROOM. A place where Jesus Christ and Judas Iscariot would be equals, with the betting odds in favor of Judas.

CREATOR. A comedian whose audience is afraid to laugh. Three proofs of His humor: democracy, hay fever, any fat woman.

DEMOCRACY. The theory that two thieves will steal less than one, and three less than two, and four less than three, and so on *ad infinitum*; the theory that the common people know what they want, and deserve to get it good and hard.

119

EPIGRAM. A platitude with vine-leaves in its hair.

EUGENICS. The theory that marriages should be made in the laboratory; the Wassermann test for love.

EVIL. That which one believes of others. It is a sin to believe evil of others, but it is seldom a mistake.

EXPERIENCE. A series of failures. Every failure teaches a man something, to wit, that he will probably fail again next time.

FAME. An embalmer trembling with stage-fright.

FINE. A bribe paid by a rich man to escape the lawful penalty of his crime. In China such bribes are paid to the judge personally; in America they are paid to him as agent for the public. But it makes no difference to the men who pay them—nor to the men who can't pay them.

FIRMNESS. A form of stupidity; proof of an inability to think the same thing out twice.

FRIENDSHIP. A mutual belief in the same fallacies, mountebanks, hobgoblins and imbecilities.

GENTLEMAN. One who never strikes a woman without provocation; one on whose word of honor the betting odds are at least 1 to 2.

HAPPINESS. Peace after effort, the overcoming of difficulties, the feeling of security and well-being. The only really happy folk are married women and single men.

HELL. A place where the Ten Commandments have a police force behind them.

HISTORIAN. An unsuccessful novelist.

HONEYMOON. The time during which the bride believes the bridegroom's word of honor.

HOPE. A pathological belief in the occurrence of the impossible.

HUMANITARIAN. One who would be sincerely sorry to see his neighbor's children devoured by wolves.

HUSBAND. One who played safe and is now played safely. A No. 16 neck in a No. 15½ collar.

HYGIENE. Bacteriology made moral; the theory that the Italian in the ditch should be jailed for spitting on his hands.

IDEALIST. One who, on noticing that a rose smells better than a cabbage, concludes that it will also make better soup.

IMMORALITY. The morality of those who are having a better time. You will never convince the average farmer's mare that the late Maud S. was not dreadfully immoral.

IMMORTALITY. The condition of a dead man who doesn't believe that he is dead.

JEALOUSY. The theory that some other fellow has just as little taste.

JUDGE. An officer appointed to mislead, restrain, hypnotize, cajole, seduce, browbeat, flabbergast and bamboozle a jury in such a manner that it will forget all the facts and give its decision to the best lawyer. The objection to judges is that they are seldom capable of a sound professional judgment of lawyers. The objection to lawyers is that the best are the worst.

JURY. A group of twelve men who, having lied to the judge about their hearing, health and business engagements, have failed to fool him.

LAWYER. One who protects us against robbers by taking away the temptation.

LIAR. (*a*) One who pretends to be very good; (*b*) one who pretends to be very bad.

LOVE. The delusion that one woman differs from another.

Love-At-First-Sight. A labor-saving device.

LOVER. An apprentice second husband; victim No. 2 in the larval stage.

MISOGYNIST. A man who hates women as much as women hate one another.

MARTYR. The husband of a woman with the martyr complex.

MORALITY. The theory that every human act must be either right or wrong, and that 99% of them are wrong.

MUSIC-LOVER. One who can tell you offhand how many sharps are in the key of C major.

OPTIMIST. The sort of man who marries his sister's best friend.

OSTEOPATH. One who argues that all human ills are caused by the pressure of hard bone upon soft tissue. The proof of his theory is to be found in the heads of those who believe it.

PASTOR. One employed by the wicked to prove to them by his example that virtue doesn't pay.

PATRIOTISM. A variety of hallucination which, if it seized a

122

bacteriologist in his laboratory, would cause him to report the streptococcus pyogenes to be as large as a Newfoundland dog, as intelligent as Socrates, as beautiful as Mont Blanc and as respectable as a Yale professor.

PENSIONER. A kept patriot.

PLATITUDE. An idea (*a*) that is admitted to be true by everyone, and (*b*) that is not true.

POLITICIAN. Any citizen with influence enough to get his old mother a job as charwoman in the City Hall.

POPULARITY. The capacity for listening sympathetically when men boast of their wives and women complain of their husbands.

POSTERITY. The penalty of a faulty technique.

PROGRESS. The process whereby the human race has got rid of whiskers, the vermiform appendix and God.

PROHIBITIONIST. The sort of man one wouldn't care to drink with, even if he drank.

PSYCHOLOGIST. One who sticks pins into babies, and then makes a chart showing the ebb and flow of their yells.

PSYCHOTHERAPY. The theory that the patient will probably get well anyhow, and is certainly a damned fool.

QUACK. A physician who has decided to admit it.

REFORMER. A hangman signing a petition against vivisection.

REMORSE. Regret that one waited so long to do it.

SELF-RESPECT. The secure feeling that no one, as yet, is suspicious.

SOB. A sound made by women, babies, tenors, fashionable clergymen, ACTORs and drunken men.

SOCIALISM. The theory that John Smith is better than his superiors.

SUICIDE. A belated acquiescence in the opinion of one's wife's relatives.

SUNDAY. A day given over by Americans to wishing that they themselves were dead and in Heaven, and that their neighbors were dead and in Hell.

SUNDAY SCHOOL. A prison in which children do penance for the evil conscience of their parents.

SURGEON. One bribed heavily by the patient to take the blame for the family doctor's error in diagnosis.

TEMPTATION. An irresistible force at work on a movable body.

THANKSGIVING DAY. A day devoted by persons with inflammatory rheumatism to thanking a loving Father that it is not hydrophobia.

THEOLOGY. An effort to explain the unknowable by putting it into terms of the not worth knowing.

TOMBSTONE. An ugly reminder of one who has been forgotten.

TRUTH. Something somehow discreditable to someone.

UNIVERSITY. A place for elevating sons above the social rank of their fathers. In the great American universities men are ranked as follows: 1. Seducers; 2. Fullbacks; 3. Booze-fighters; 4. Pitchers and Catchers; 5. Poker players; 6. Scholars; 7. Christians.

VERDICT. The *a priori* opinion of that juror who smokes the worst cigars.

VERS LIBRE. A device for making poetry easier to write and harder to read.

WART. Something that outlasts ten thousand kisses.

WEALTH. Any income that is at least $100 more a year than the income of one's wife's sister's husband.

WEDDING. A device for exciting envy in women and terror in men.

WIFE. One who is sorry she did it, but would undoubtedly do it again.

WIDOWER. One released on parole.

WOMAN. Before marriage, an *agente provocateuse*; after marriage, a *gendarme*.

WOMEN'S CLUB. A place in which the validity of a philosophy is judged by the hat of its prophetess.

YACHT CLUB. An asylum for landsmen who would rather die of drink than be seasick.

XII

The Old Subject

§ 1.

Men have a much better time of it than women. For one thing, they marry later. For another thing, they die earlier.

§ 2.

The man who marries for love alone is at least honest. But so was Czolgosz.

§ 3.

When a husband's story is believed, he begins to suspect his wife.

§ 4.

In the year 1830 the average American had six children and one wife. How time transvalues all values!

§ 5.

Love begins like a triolet and ends like a college yell.

§ 6.

A man always blames the woman who fools him. In the same way he blames the door he walks into in the dark.

§ 7.

Man's objection to love is that it dies hard; woman's is that when it is dead it stays dead.

§ 8.

Definition of a good mother: one who loves her child almost as much as a little girl loves her doll.

§ 9.

The way to hold a husband is to keep him a little bit jealous. The way to lose him is to keep him a little bit more jealous.

§ 10.

It used to be thought in America that a woman ceased to be a lady the moment her name appeared in a newspaper. It is no longer thought so, but it is still true.

§ 11.

Women have simple tastes. They can get pleasure out of the conversation of children in arms and men in love.

§ 12.

Whenever a husband and wife begin to discuss their marriage they are giving evidence at a coroner's inquest.

§ 13.

How little it takes to make life unbearable!... A pebble in the shoe, a cockroach in the spaghetti, a woman's laugh!

§ 14.

The bride at the altar: "At last! At last!" THE BRIDEGROOM: "Too late! Too late!"

§ 15.

The best friend a woman can have is the man who has got over loving her. He would rather die than compromise her.

§ 16.

The one breathless passion of every woman is to get some one married. If she's single, it's herself. If she's married, it's the woman her husband would probably marry if she died tomorrow.

§ 17.

Man weeps to think that he will die so soon. Woman, that she was born so long ago.

§ 18.

Woman is at once the serpent, the apple—and the belly-ache.

§ 19.

Cold mutton-stew; a soiled collar; breakfast in dress clothes; a wet house-dog, over-affectionate; the other fellow's tooth-brush; an echo of "Ta-ra-ra-boom-de-ay"; the damp, musty smell of an empty house; stale beer; a mangy fur coat; *Katzenjammer*; false teeth; the criticism of Hamilton Wright Mabie; boiled cabbage; a cocktail *after* dinner; an old cigar butt; ... the kiss of Evelyn after the inauguration of Eleanor.

§ 20.

Whenever a woman begins to talk of anything, she is talking to, of, or at a man.

§ 21.

The worst man hesitates when choosing a mother for his children. And hesitating, he is lost.

§ 22.

Women always excel men in that sort of wisdom which comes from experience. To be a woman is in itself a terrible experience.

§ 23.

No man is ever too old to look at a woman, and no woman is ever too fat to hope that he will look.

§ 24.

Bachelors have consciences. Married men have wives.

§ 25.

Bachelors know more about women than married men. If they did't they'd be married, too.

§ 26.

Man is a natural polygamist. He always has one woman leading him by the nose and another hanging on to his coat-tails.

§ 27.

All women, soon or late, are jealous of their daughters; all men, soon or late, are envious of their sons.

§ 28.

History seems to bear very harshly upon women. One cannot recall more than three famous women who were virtuous. But on turning to famous men the seeming injustice disappears. One would have difficulty finding even two of them who were virtuous.

§ 29.

Husbands never become good; they merely become proficient.

§ 30.

Strike an average between what a woman thinks of her husband a month before she marries him and what she thinks of him a year afterward, and you will have the truth about him in a very handy form.

§ 31.

The worst of marriage is that it makes a woman believe that all men are just as easy to fool.

§ 32.

The great secret of happiness in love is to be glad that the other fellow married her.

§ 33.

A man may be a fool and not know it—but not if he is married.

§ 34.

All men are proud of their own children. Some men carry egoism so far that they are even proud of their own wives.

§ 35.

When you sympathize with a married woman you either make two enemies or gain one wife and one friend.

§ 36.

Women do not like timid men. Cats do not like prudent rats.

§ 37.

He marries best who puts it off until it is too late.

§ 38.

A bachelor is one who wants a wife, but is glad he hasn't got her.

§ 40.

Women usually enjoy annoying their husbands, but not when they annoy them by growing fat.

XIII

Panoramas of People

I

Men

Fat, slick, round-faced men, of the sort who haunt barber shops and are always having their shoes shined. Tall, gloomy, Gothic men, with eyebrows that meet over their noses and bunches of black, curly hair in their ears. Men wearing diamond solitaires, fraternal order watchcharms, golden elks' heads with rubies for eyes. Men with thick, loose lips and shifty eyes. Men smoking pale, spotted cigars. Men who do not know what to do with their hands when they talk to women. Honorable, upright, successful men who seduce their stenographers and are kind to their dear old mothers. Men who allow their wives to dress like chorus girls. White-faced, scared-looking, yellow-eyed men who belong to societies for the suppression of vice. Men who boast that they neither drink nor smoke. Men who mop their bald heads with perfumed handkerchiefs. Men with drawn, mottled faces, in the last stages of arterio-sclerosis. Silent, stupid-looking men in thick tweeds who tramp up and down the decks of ocean steamers. Men who peep out of hotel rooms at Swedish chambermaids. Men who go to church on Sunday morning, carrying Oxford Bibles under their arms. Men in dress coats too tight under the arms. Tea-drinking men. Loud, back-slapping men, gabbling endlessly about baseball players. Men who have never heard of Mozart. Tired business men with fat, glittering wives. Men who know what to do when children are sick. Men who believe that any woman who smokes is a prostitute. Yellow, diabetic men. Men whose veins are on the outside of their noses. Now and then a clean, clear-eyed, upstanding man. Once a week or so a man with good shoulders, straight legs and a hard, resolute mouth....

II

Women

Fat women with flabby, double chins. Moon-faced, pop-eyed women in little flat hats. Women with starchy faces and thin vermilion lips. Man-shy, suspicious women, shrinking into their clothes every time a wet, caressing eye alights upon them. Women soured and robbed of their souls by Christian Endeavor. Women who would probably be members of the Lake Mohonk Conference if they were men. Gray-haired, middle-aged, waddling women, wrecked and unsexed by endless, useless parturition, nursing, worry, sacrifice. Women who look as if they were still innocent yesterday afternoon. Women in shoes that bend their insteps to preposterous semi-circles. Women with green, barbaric bangles in their ears, like the concubines of Arab horse-thieves. Women looking in show-windows, wishing that their husbands were not such poor sticks. Shapeless women lolling in six thousand dollar motorcars. Trig little blondes, stepping like Shetland ponies. Women smelling of musk, ambergris, bergamot. Long-legged, cadaverous, hungry women. Women eager to be kidnapped, betrayed, forced into marriage at the pistol's point. Soft, pulpy, pale women. Women with ginger-colored hair and large, irregular freckles. Silly, chattering, gurgling women. Women showing their ankles to policemen, chauffeurs, street-cleaners. Women with slim-shanked, whining, sticky-fingered children dragging after them.

Women marching like grenadiers. Yellow women. Women with red hands. Women with asymmetrical eyes. Women with rococo ears. Stoop-shouldered women. Women with huge hips. Bow-legged women. Appetizing women. Good-looking women....

III

Babies

Babies smelling of camomile tea, cologne water, wet laundry, dog soap, *Schmierkase*. Babies who appear old, disillusioned and tired of life at six months. Babies that cry "Papa!" to blushing youths of nineteen or twenty at church picnics. Fat babies whose earlobes turn out at an angle of forty-five degrees. Soft, pulpy babies asleep in perambulators, the sun shining straight into their faces. Babies gnawing the tails of synthetic dogs. Babies without necks. Pale, scorbutic babies of the third and fourth generation, damned because their grandfathers and great-grandfathers read Tom Paine. Babies of a bluish tinge, or with vermilion eyes. Babies full of soporifics. Thin, cartilaginous babies that stretch when they are lifted. Warm, damp, miasmatic babies. Affectionate, ingratiating, gurgling babies: the *larvæ* of life insurance solicitors, fashionable doctors, Episcopal rectors, dealers in Mexican mine stock, handshakers, Sunday-school superintendents. Hungry babies, absurdly sucking their thumbs. Babies with heads of thick, coarse black hair, seeming to be toupees. Unbaptized babies, dedicated to the devil. Eugenic babies. Babies that crawl out from under tables and are stepped on. Babies with lintels, grains of corn or shoe-buttons up their noses, purple in the face and waiting for the doctor or the embalmer. A few pink, blue-eyed, tight-skinned, clean-looking babies, smiling upon the world....

XIV

Homeopathics

1.
Scene Infernal.

During a lull in the uproar of Hell two voices were heard.

"My name," said one, "was Ludwig van Beethoven. I was no ordinary musician. The Archduke Rudolph used to speak to me on the streets of Vienna."

"And mine," said the other, "was the Archduke Rudolph. I was no ordinary archduke. Ludwig van Beethoven dedicated a trio to me."

2.
The Eternal Democrat.

A Socialist, carrying a red flag, marched through the gates of Heaven.

"To Hell with rank!" he shouted. "All men are equal here."

Just then the late Karl Marx turned a corner and came into view, meditatively stroking his whiskers. At once the Socialist fell upon his knees and touched his forehead to the dust.

"O Master!" he cried. "O Master, Master!"

3.

The School of Honor.

A trembling young reporter stood in the presence of an eminent city editor.

"If I write this story," said the reporter, "it will rob a woman of her good name."

"If you don't write it," said the city editor, "I'll give you a kick in the pantaloons."

Next day the young reporter got a raise in salary and the woman swallowed two ounces of permanganate of potassium.

4.

Proposed Plot For a Modern Novel.

Herman was in love with Violet, the wife of Armand, an elderly diabetic. Armand showed three per cent of sugar a day. Herman and Violet, who were Christians, awaited with virtuous patience the termination of Armand's distressing malady.

One day Dr. Frederick M. Allen discovered his cure for diabetes.

5.

Victory.

"I wooed and won her," said the Man of His Wife.

"I made him run," said the Hare of the Hound.

XV

Vers Libre

Kiss me on the other eye; This one's wearing out.